D1328920

3 4114 00410 5556

THE BAKER'S APPRENTICE

Molly Mason dreams of escaping from the suffocating existence of life with her stepmother, Mrs Cecily Creswell and her daughter Juniper. She plans to make her escape by becoming an apprentice to her friend the local baker, Alice Arndale. However, when Juniper's fiancé Lt. Cherry, a war hero, returns home early, he arrives with Mr Julian Creswell, a missing soldier, presumed dead — and Julian brings with him suspicions of murder, mystery and the key to Molly's heart . . .

VALERIE HOLMES

THE BAKER'S APPRENTICE

Complete and Unabridged

LINFORD
Leicester

First published in Great Britain in 2008

First Linford Edition
published 2009

British Library CIP Data

Holmes, Valerie.
  The baker's apprentice - -
  (Linford romance library)
  1. Stepfamilies- -Fiction. 2. Soldiers- -Fiction.
  3. Love stories. 4. Large type books.
  I. Title II. Series
  823.9′2–dc22

  ISBN 978–1–84782–755–5

Published by
F. A. Thorpe (Publishing)
Anstey, Leicestershire

Set by Words & Graphics Ltd.
Anstey, Leicestershire
Printed and bound in Great Britain by
T. J. International Ltd., Padstow, Cornwall

This book is printed on acid-free paper

*A friend suggested that I hadn't written
a story which began in a shop . . .*

Now I have . . .

Dedicated to . . .
<u>*Mrs Vivienne Bass*</u>

1

'Molly Mason! What do you think you're doing there, lass?' Alice returned from the cellar of the bakery, red faced, and stared at the well-dressed young woman in her shop. She was busy arranging a batch of quartern loaves neatly in the window display of the small, yet prolific, bakery. The pies on the shelves had already been placed for her in neat rows.

'Hello there, Mrs Arndale.' Molly turned around quickly, smiling at the woman she adored as her friend and confidant. With a slightly guilty look in her eye she discreetly placed the empty bread basket out of the way, as she thought, behind the counter.

'Molly, how many times do I have to tell you to keep your hands off my bread, pies and cakes? If your ma should walk by and see you fussing over my window display you'll be banned from coming here.' She bent over and lifted up the basket, placing it on a shelf above the cellar stairs. 'I don't know . . . Even leaving stuff lying around for me to fall headlong over!' The woman tutted at her, but Molly Mason ignored her friendly protestations.

'She isn't my mother, Mrs Arndale, as you know fine well. Besides, what would Mrs Cecily Creswell be doing walking past your window?' Molly held her head high and sniffed as though there was a foul smell under her nose.

Alice laughed at her.

'You also know,' Molly continued in her normal manner, 'that she'd ban me from breathing if she thought it gave me pleasure, so what should I care what she thinks?' Molly laughed as she remembered the latest character flaw of hers that Cecily had taken pains over dinner to discuss in front of her own daughter, Juniper. 'You see I have already been told not to smile too much when I am in the town in case people think I'm simple, or heaven forbid, I encourage the 'wrong sort' of attention.' She looked back with satisfaction at the display she had just created. The still warm bread was arranged on a piece of cloth that she had sewn into a square especially for it. She showed no interest or talent with a needle when it came to embroidering samplers, and what she considered useless frippery, but for the practical things in life, like making clothes, she had a natural eye and talent for it.

Her stepmother had presumed, wrongly, that because she had no interest in needlepoint she was useless at it, which was just as well, or else she would have put Molly's talent to work for her in the woman's own establishment.

'Molly! Molly Creswell!'

'Mason! Molly Mason! I shall have my father's name even if that woman prefers to keep that of her first husband.' Molly's lips were set firm.

'It is the name of her business; it

makes sense, I suppose. People think of you as her daughter and not that of a cobbler from another town. It's not meant as a slight. That mouth of yours will have you in deep trouble before you're much older. She is your mother now because she married your father. You best learn to accept the fact. You cannot deny that he benefited grand style from wooing and wedding Cecily Creswell. He'd sold up and moved into that new terraced house of hers as soon as it was finished. Quite the gentleman he was.'

'Father was a gentleman. He worked hard all his life.'

'Aye, he did that. My sister lived over Beckton way. Had a soft spot for Eli, she did. Shame, though, that Cecily saw him out, and not the other way round.' Alice Arndale added the last comment in a quieter, softly spoken voice.

'She saw him out . . . or finished him off,' Molly said bitterly.

'Now then, lass! That's dangerous and wicked talk. You know they were

4

suited to each other well enough. Both had education, so harness that attitude or it will be your undoing.'

Mrs Alice Arndale seated her ample bottom on her stool and rubbed the flour from her hands; she then placed her cloth cap upon her head and exchanged her soiled apron for a nice clean one.

'Are you expecting Mr Gossage this morning?' Molly asked, and could not help herself from smiling as Alice's ruddy cheeks flushed even deeper.

'I'll turf you out if you get insolent with me. Now what does 'Lady' Cecily require from the lowly baker woman today?' She was changing the subject swiftly.

Molly held out a list to her, hesitated, and said, 'Sorry, Mrs Arndale, I forgot. I'll read it out for you.'

'You don't need to be 'sorry', lass,' Alice snapped a little haughtily, as the note was snatched out of Molly's hand. 'I know me goods and I know me numbers. So unless she's taken to writing to me, all chatty like, then I will easily find out what she wants.' Alice stared at the paper and screwed up her face as she struggled with the words.

'Alice, Mrs Arndale, why don't you let me teach you how to read . . . ' Molly's words were out of her mouth before she had thought about what she was saying to her. Alice was an excellent baker, friend and an all round good person in Molly's eyes. However, she was proud and illiterate.

Alice stood up; Molly stepped back against the wood panelled wall as a stubby finger was pointed at her. 'I run a business here, like my mother afore me. It may not be as grand as 'Creswell's Millinery and Dresses for ladies of refinement' but I put food into empty bellies. I charge a fair price for quality,' she glanced at the bread, 'and that ain't easy because of the cost of me flour now. Anyway, why should I need to waste my time mulling over letters?' She placed both fists on her hips and waited for Molly to reply. I have a friend who sees to that side of things for me.

'Because then you would be able to do more to help your business and read the orders out easily, saving you precious time and mistakes, instead of struggling on with fading sight. It's one thing that holds you, a fine woman, back. Cecily isn't a better person than you, or better at business for that matter, but she is educated, and that helps her. You could do better, Mrs Arndale ... You know you could.' Molly stood straight and stared at the speechless woman opposite.

'I haven't the time,' she replied, as she sat down and tossed Molly a small pie.

Molly caught it in her gloved hand. 'Then make it!' she said simply, and took a bite of the pie, loving the fresh taste of the meaty middle.

'Ha! You think I can act like God?' she said quickly, then nervously looked around her and crossed herself. 'No one can stop time still. Now, end your

7

nonsense, I have work to do. So you best be about your own and I'll get on with mine.' She glanced out of the bay window and looked a little disappointed.

'Why not hire an apprentice?' Molly asked innocently, as she brushed the crumbs from her gloves.

'An apprentice . . . why? I manage fine.' Alice shook her head; her cap flopped around her sandy hair. 'No, it wouldn't work well. I work on my own. I'm best that way. I've standards to keep up.' Alice sniffed the air a little. 'Besides, Sally helps me watch the ovens and does my deliveries for me.'

'She's a sweet young girl but she is no apprentice and never will be.' Molly was speaking low. 'She'll be married in a year or so and then where will you be? That one is a nester not a worker. She likes the boys.'

Alice sighed deeply. 'You are so hard sometimes. She's not got the most peas in the pod but she works well enough. You don't need to feel sorry for me.'

'If you worked with someone you could trust and who trusted you, then the work would not stand in the way of the learning.' Molly saw a smile cross her friend's face.

'Cecily Creswell would have a fit. A daughter of her house working as an apprentice in a baker shop in Lower Lane, when she owns a fine establishment in the High Lane.' Her head shook with even more commitment. 'No, she'd never allow it. There'd be nought but trouble for us both.' Alice looked genuinely worried.

'Why? Her own daughter is her apprentice at the milliners' shop. Juniper is always at 'Mama's' side. She can do no wrong and clearly is being trained to take over the establishment, whilst Cecily hunts down her next victim to marry . . . Herbert Gossage, perhaps?'

'You have a sharp and ugly tongue in that young head of yours when you want to use it. Herbert is no fool. He didn't bring that business of his to the fine coach house it is without his head on right, girl.' Her cheeks flushed again. Alice had a soft spot for the man, but Molly had seen him use his banter with Cecily and she was a woman of ambition. A fine coach house would be a good match to her establishment. Both dealt with finery for the more affluent in the region. Now the roads had been remade with the new smoother surfaces, the region was starting to encourage more strangers into it. Cecily read the news sheets and planned. Her business had not succeeded purely by chance ... she thought.

'He's a man, Alice. They don't think like us.' Molly looked quite serious at her friend but Alice suddenly burst into fits of laughter.

'You sound like a jaded old biddy and you not even been wed yet.' Alice dabbed the corner of her eyes with her handkerchief.

Molly ignored her. The fact that she had such a low opinion of men was the main reason why she had refused to be matched off before now. 'She cannot stop it then. I have my birthday tomorrow and she has forgotten all about it because Juniper's young man is coming to stay with us, and I am to make myself scarce so that they have 'time' together to become better acquainted as they finalise their plans; with Cecily, of course. So, you see, I can decide for myself, whilst she plans to wed me over to Joshua Salmon in the spring.'

'What that sluggard? His dad may own the inn but he's not a good or kindly man, Molly. You should do better. Take my warning. He is the sort who would break a strong spirited woman; stay away from him.' She sighed deeply. 'Well, then, you have as usual won me over to the possibility of seeing the world from your eyes, so come back tomorrow with your things and I shall make up me spare room for you. But Molly, she will be vexed and she is a woman of some influence and means. Don't you scupper me liveli-hood just to spite that bitch.' Molly stared at her earnestly.

'I won't, but there is one more thing I need from you tomorrow. I need to see Mr Gubbins of Haithwaite & Goole, in private. They were Father's solicitors and the man sent me a note to meet him tomorrow in a convenient and neutral place.' Molly looked at her with a sparkle to her eye.

'You think your father may have left you an inheritance separate to Cecily's?' Alice replied enthusiastically.

'Possibly, but I shall not read too much into it, but I need . . . ' she stepped forwards.

'You've told him to meet you here, haven't you?' Alice raised her eyebrow.

'Can I use your parlour at one o'clock?' Molly was leaning on the counter anxiously looking at Alice's face.

'Yes, but please keep me out of any bother.' Alice glanced out of the window and suddenly became all of a fluster. 'Now you get along and I'll see you tomorrow . . . we shall talk then.'

The door opened and the fine figure of Herbert Gossage entered the bakery. He was quite tall with a bearded face, a happy disposition and a hearty girth. Herbert enjoyed his lifestyle and Alice's pies.

Molly nodded goodbye to Alice and exchanged greetings with Mr Gossage, then quickly stepped outside leaving a very happy Alice to welcome her regular customer inside.

Tomorrow would be a new beginning and whatever this Mr Gubbins had to tell her, Molly prayed it would in some way set her free of Cecily's patronage, for she loathed the woman.

2

Molly made her way reluctantly back toward the milliner's shop in High Lane. Here the town was taking on a new look. The muddy track of a road that had existed for much of the small town's existence was now covered in the new style. The houses were high and regular in design and the bay fronted shops were impressive. Cecily had purchased the larger double bay-fronted premises with the window panes larger than any Molly had seen before. She represented the new world. The old, the poor would be crushed, removed and lost.

Molly looked stylish in her cream walking dress, green velvet spencer, with matching hat and gloves, but she had no love or patience for the idle gossip that she knew would greet her inside. Her raven hair and complexion contrasted dramatically with the fabric to fine effect.

She breathed in deeply as her hand found the handle of the shop door and she boldly stepped inside Cecily's place.

'Mrs Dodsley, Mary has arrived just in time to show you just how flattering the à la grecque' style of walking dress is on a young figure.' Cecily turned to her with one hand raised. 'Come, Mary, remove the Spencer and show Mrs Dodsley how splendid your new dress is.' She smiled sweetly, but Molly thought that it was a smile that could freeze a heart rather than melt one with the warmth of human kindness. It grated on her to be called by her birth name, Mary. It was one she had shared with her mother, and her father had insisted she became Molly after her mother died. It was to be a new start for both of them and so they had lived and loved each other through an empty dark time emerging as Molly and Eli, instead of Mary and Elijah. It had suited them well for three precious years until her father had decided to move on one step further and courted Cecily. He was a clever, educated man with an eye on the politics of the time. Molly had to admit he left her in a good home. Perhaps he even realised his own health would not hold.

She removed her coat and gloves, showing the long line of the high-waisted dress. It suited her and she did like it. Cecily had skill and taste, she admitted reluctantly to herself.

'I'm not sure it will suit her, Cecily. It is rather . . . plain! And she is so delicate in stature.' Mrs Dodsley looked rather nervous as Mrs Creswell's eyes half closed, her dark eyes still managing to give a penetrating stare. Meanwhile, Molly tried to keep a straight face, stifling a smile, as to call one of her garments plain was a little short-sighted if not insulting.

'Plain? Plain?' Mrs Creswell repeated, bringing a hand up to her chest as if a sudden pain had shot through her. She glanced to her beloved daughter for support, which was instantly given. Juniper sat primly in the corner of the room, her fair hair perfectly dressed as if she was at a ball. The ringlets that cascaded by her fair cheeks did nothing to enliven what was unquestionably a plain face. Possibly her best feature, referred to by her mother as a Romanesque nose, Molly tended to think of as big, but she would have loved her as a sister if her heart had been in earnest; unfortunately her mother had passed on most of her own values to the girl.

'Have you ever heard such a comment before, Juniper? To say any of my garments are plain shows that the classical style does not perhaps rate in your traditional view of fashion!'

Juniper shook her head so that her curls bobbed frantically about her pale cheeks. 'No, Mother, indeed I have not. For it is the fashion at its best.' The girl walked over to Molly.

'Mrs Dodsley, if you look at the close fitting here. See how the quality muslin is gathered in surplice style — neck and shoulders perfected to show the ample cleavage to its best; so even a country sort of girl can be improved; shown to their best advantage by the cut of the garment. No stitch has been made in haste or by a clumsy hand. Our garments are pieces of art, ma'am. Plain is not a word that does them justice, yet in the straight line, the eye applauds the uncluttered simplicity of the quality and style. In short, ma'am, this garment is nothing short of perfection itself.'

Mrs Creswell smiled broadly at her daughter for she had trained her well. 'Indeed, if anything is plain it is the wearer, and not the dress!'

Juniper was now very confident. When she had her mother's approval she was brave around Molly. Her stepmother called her Mary as she had decided that Molly sounded like the name of a milkmaid. Molly had immediately pointed out that it was the name of a chosen woman to carry a special gift to the world. The slap she received was the one and only one she ever had accepted for her insolence. From that moment no bond would ever be formed to secure a harmonious relationship between the two women.

Juniper pointed to the waistline which Molly thought would have been the neckline if her bust had not been in the way; for the skirt was as long as it could be. The tight fit of the garment hugged her breasts closely and accentuated her fullness, whilst the square cut of the neckline itself exposed her cleavage more than Molly preferred. Molly had therefore chosen to wear the gauze collar that could be fitted in a criss-cross fashion, meeting at a point behind the neck, providing modest apparel. The effect was more to Molly's taste.

Juniper, however, needed all the help she could get to accentuate her naturally flat state and envied Molly. This was another reason why Molly could not wait to leave their house. It had never felt like a home to her since they moved there when her father remarried.

'If we remove this,' Juniper released the gauze, 'you can see that on the right girl this dress of perfect simplicity and excellent craftsmanship would turn the eye of any young man.' She looked at Mrs Dodsley who seemed to be swayed by her words.

Molly stepped back from Juniper's interfering hands. She looked at Mrs Dodsley's slightly troubled face and smiled. 'Is it for young Agnes, for the summer ball at the Assembly rooms next month?' she asked.

'Why, yes, actually it is, Ma . . . Molly,' the woman answered, looking relieved that Molly had spoken to her directly.

'Then may I suggest that you have one made for her in the lightest of colours as she is quite short and slim. Then she should appear a little more ample. It is indeed comfortable to wear and I'm sure she would like it.' Molly wrapped the gauze back around her neckline and retrieved her spencer.

'Oh, thank you, Molly. I feel certain she will look grand in it, young Juniper explained it so well.' She nodded to both mother and daughter then stared at Molly directly. 'Will you call on us tomorrow?' the woman said enthusiastically.

'Yes, tomorrow afternoon . . . late afternoon, if that would be fine with you?'

'Yes . . . ' Mrs Dodsley began.

'Splendid, I'll have Mr Gossage send a coach to take the girls over to your residence at . . . say, at two. Will that be in order?' Cecily stepped in and Juniper smiled broadly because she loved visiting.

Mrs Dodsley looked slightly crestfallen. 'Splendid, would two be suitable for you, Molly?'

'Of course it will be,' Cecily counted. 'What else has the wastrel to do with her time? It is Juniper whose industrious nature will have to be torn away from her designs.' Cecily exchanged knowing smiles with her daughter, and Molly knew there would only be more trouble if she raised their suspicions and disagreed with their plans.

'That would be fine, Mrs Dodsley.' Molly excused herself and left, adding to her prayers that, whatever Mr Gubbins had to tell her, he would be able to do it swiftly. However, she realised that all depended on what was said for, in truth, if she was to be independent of Cecily, she need not be in the coach at all. With that happy thought she made her way back to her room, her sanctuary.

3

The conversation over dinner had been all about the attitude of the 'ignorant' Mrs Dodsley, who knew nothing of modern styles or appreciated the quality of their garments. In the eyes of Juniper and Cecily she was an uneducated country woman. Their diatribe went on and on whilst Molly ate her fill of dinner, lost most of the time in her own thoughts; namely, what she could wear to meet Mr Gubbins in a formal capacity tomorrow afternoon, and then how to go straight on for a social outing to see her friend Agnes. She hoped Mrs Dodsley would involve Juniper in some decision-making process on her wardrobe, as she tactfully did so often, whilst Molly and her friend managed to indulge in some tittle-tattle of their own interest.

'Don't you agree, Mary?' Cecily's

voice cut through her thoughts like a knife.

'Yes . . . sorry, I was daydreaming.' She smiled sweetly at the two disgruntled faces in front of her.

'We were talking about the importance of events tomorrow,' Cecily explained, and Molly felt her stomach knot as she dared to imagine what events in particular they were referring to. Cecily did not appear to notice and continued, 'When the young Lt. arrives tomorrow.' Cecily smiled as Juniper blushed slightly.

Molly was not so easily impressed. However, she did think that Lt. Ambrose Cherry was as wet behind the ears as his proposed beloved so, she thought rather mischievously, they should be a perfect match for each other and suitable puppets for Cecily to rule over. His father was in fading health, so the opposition for control of the couple was also weak. Cecily, Molly appreciated, planned very well indeed.

Cecily continued, 'He will not reach

here until the early evening. He is travelling by post-chaise. So keen is he to see his dear Juniper that he will arrive fresh from port, so we shall make sure that our hero has a fitting and homely welcome.'

'And a comfortable bed ready for him to collapse in to as soon as the need is there,' Molly added.

'Yes, of course. That goes without saying, which is why I suppose you did — always the obvious, Mary. So tell me, girl, pray what were you so rudely daydreaming about ... Mr Salmon, perhaps?' She lifted a glass of wine to her lips and sipped it slowly. Over the years that Molly had known her, she had noticed how the lines had deepened and her facial powder thickened. Her figure was still straight and youthful, though, for her years.

'No, ma'am, I never waste my thoughts on him.' Molly stared straight back at Cecily who she could see was humoured by her show of spirit, but it was one she had always underestimated like her sewing abilities.

'Mama! That is the word that would soothe my ears. When shall I hear that title spoken from your mouth, girl? Do I not feed and clothe you, Mary? I use your birth name, unlike most others. Are you not treated like my very own, dear Juniper, yet you keep a void between us. You have no notion how much you hurt me . . . deeply, child.' She took another sip and Juniper reached out her own hand and patted her mother's free one gently. Cecily smiled at the gesture, but Molly just looked on blankly, without envy or feeling at their show of closeness.

'I do not mean to hurt, ma'am. However, I hope you will understand that it is out of respect to my own mother that I reserve the title uniquely for her, posthumously of course.' Molly glanced humbly down at her own cupped hands upon her lap when she had an idea. 'I was just thinking, if tomorrow I wore the new coat dress from the display, the burgundy one made in the military style, over my walking dress, I might be able to convince Mrs Dodsley to order one for Agnes. With Juniper's help, of course. She describes the finery better than I do, and I so love wearing it.'

'Of course, that is an excellent idea. Juniper had said something similar earlier, but the burgundy coat dress is too long for her. Yes, you may try it, but replace it on the dummy with the blue cloak.' Cecily was calculating the profit to be made; Molly could tell by her distracted manner. So Molly took the moment to escape and stood up, anxious to leave.

'Where are you going, Molly?' Cecily asked.

'Oh, I thought I would like to sort out my apparel for tomorrow,' Molly smiled enthusiastically.

'My! My! We may not want to work for our keep. However, we are keen to display the latest goods. Tell me, Molly Manson, are you showing any young man your favour? I hope you are not indulging in a *tête à tête*.' Cecily placed her crystal wine glass carefully back down on the table and stared at Molly directly.

'No! Absolutely not . . . no one, I assure you. I have no interest in marrying just yet.' She tried to smile but was surprised when Cecily did not even pretend to smile back.

'Reputations are like the finest, most delicate silk, beautiful whilst intact yet so ugly when their beauty is damaged — one slight stain, girl, and they are so easily destroyed. Just one stain, Mary, and you'll be ruined.'

'There is no one, I swear!' Molly exclaimed, trying to regain her normally calm composure.

'You are so unusual for a girl . . . no, that is not correct, for I should be saying for a woman of your age. For tomorrow will be a double celebration. We have a Lieutenant arriving for my Juniper and you, Mary, become a woman in numbers only. So we shall have to plan something for you also.

Perhaps we should invite Mr Salmon to join us for dinner to balance the table.' Cecily's eyes almost gleamed in the darkened lamp-lit room. She had not forgotten the birthday date, but Molly was sure that she did not know about Mr Gubbins' request for a meeting.

'It would be a waste of his time, ma'am, for I have no wish to marry a man who drinks to excess.' Molly was now standing by the door. 'I would rather marry a man of temperance.'

Cecily laughed out loud. 'Then you shall indeed die an old maid. Take my advice, girl, grab the best you can whilst you still can. Life for a single woman is hard. Now go and play with your frippery and I shall see you tomorrow at the shop at twenty minutes to two, sharp. The coach will be waiting.'

Molly nodded and left them, wondering if it were possible to be at the appointment at one o'clock, and with Cecily forty minutes later. She almost forgot that she had arranged to move in with Alice as her apprentice, to escape from Cecily's plans. Molly realised that she had acted in haste. The bakery was where she would rather be; yet, there were benefits to living in the comfortable house and with the pick of the fashion. She displayed Cecily's clothes well, which was why she was allowed to wear them and go about town in style. But her heart wanted to be with Alice, for she was the closest person to her on earth.

Molly took the key for the shop and let herself out of the back of the house. Wrapped in a large black cloak she made her way down to the establishment, deciding to swap the burgundy coat as instructed and have it done with, so she did not have to enter the shop the following morning, risking being drawn into some task for Cecily which would set her plans askew.

It was darker outside than she had anticipated. Every doorway was accentuated by the blackness of the shadow. Molly experienced a growing feeling that her judgement on this occasion could have been better.

She placed the key in the door's lock as quickly as she could. Her fingers were cold and her hand was shaking for some reason. Nervously, she placed the burgundy coat in a roll under her coat. She did not want to waste any time so quickly replaced it with the other garment, then locked the door behind her. She could hear her heart pounding in her chest. Why did she feel like a thief in the night?

She turned to make her way back along the moonlit street when a hand grabbed her shoulder and spun her around as if she were no more than a rag doll.

'What on earth do we have here?' The deep voice caused her to let out a gasp as she was faced with a gentleman in riding apparel, holding a crop in his other hand. She had considered kicking him but saw the crop and thought better of it.

'You have nothing here. Sir, why should you accost a woman in the street in such a manner? Are you trying to scare me half to death?' Molly stood straight and stared at his hand. 'Remove it, please!'

He smiled broadly at her. 'I could arrest you as a thief, but what thief has her own key? So I could assume you are a dishonest employee, but then,' with the end of his crop he opened one side of her cloak, 'what thief dresses for dinner in such quality cloth first? So tell me, miss, who are you and what is it you are about at this hour, or I shall have you booked in for the next assizes for 'simple grand larceny.'' He tapped the rolled up coat with the crop.

Molly, scared and furious in equal measure, exclaimed loudly and clearly, 'How dare you imply such a foul slur upon my character! Why would I steal at all from my own establishment?'

'Why indeed?' he asked, but did not remove his hand.

4

It was with much indignation that Molly was walked over to where he had left his horse. Another man held the animal's reins in his hand and Molly was most surprised to see the face of Juniper's Lieutenant looking down at her. He was somewhat changed in appearance. His smooth, clear skin was different, stubbly, and his eyes no longer had that vacant optimism they possessed before he went away to be a hero for the King and country.

'Mary Mason?' He said her name, yet was clearly asking her if she was the person who he thought he recognised.

'Lieutenant, if you know this annoying person would you be so kind as to ask him to remove his hand from my shoulder!' Her words were sharp, but really she was feeling very uncomfortable and realised that she could be in a great deal of trouble. Nothing, at the moment, was more important to Cecily's plans than announcing to the world the match between this young man and her daughter. Yet, here she, Molly, was being almost arrested in the street as a thief by him and his friend. It was totally embarrassing and not the impression that Cecily would have her make.

The man released her shoulder and stood quite relaxed by her side. In his military coat he looked both tall and menacing to her.

'Lieutenant, I apologise for meeting you in the street in such a ridiculous manner.' She glanced up at the stranger next to her with what she hoped was a good impersonation of Cecily's condemning stare, only to see a face lit up by amusement. 'We expected you to arrive tomorrow evening.'

'Yes, Miss Mason, I am fully aware of our arrangements so may I make a suggestion?' he leaned forward and whispered to her, 'It might be in both our interests, miss, if you say nothing of this unfortunate meeting and I shall keep my silence also. That way you can return home safely, without disturbing Mrs Creswell's rest and I shall have time to find a suitable room in which to bathe and make myself more presentable for my arrival tomorrow evening. Is that idea conducive to you?' He winked at her rather annoyingly. However, Molly could see how his proposition would benefit both.

'An excellent idea, sir. Now if you'll excuse me I shall return home.' She turned to leave and was surprised when the stranger spoke out.

'I'll see you to your door. If Lt. Cherry, will take the horse to the inn, I'll join you and Herbert there.' The man stepped up alongside her on the newly laid paving and waited for her to join him.

'I am perfectly able to walk myself home, sir.' Molly looked up at him seeing that the humour was not completely gone from his face.

Cherry left them, taking the stranger's horse as he was ordered. He obviously expected the man to have his way.

'No, miss, you cannot. Not safely. I could have been a cut-throat or a thief . . . or worse.' His countenance became more serious.

'You are trying to scare me unnecessarily,' she replied, and walked on.

He ambled along by her side, uninvited.

'Tell me, miss, how often you walk the streets at night?' he asked, and the he stopped as she did.

'I do not like what you are implying. I am no . . . it was an unusual circumstance that brought me to the shop at this hour. We live quite near as you are aware and I did not see what harm I could possibly find myself in on such a short errand. I do not walk the streets at this hour at all!' She was keeping her voice low but the annoyance was still clear within her words.

'Miss, if anyone should look out of

the windows of these respectable homes and witness you and I strolling out together your reputation would crumble. Did you not stop and think about the consequences of your actions at all, lest they do not run to plan?' His voice sounded almost incredulous.

'I . . . I didn't expect you to accost me.' She pulled him into the shadow of an alley way. It was dark now and she felt foolish. 'I shall admit I made an error of judgement. I didn't think . . . not clearly. I did something stupid. You have made your point clearly, sir. Now if you would escort me down here and around the back of these terraces, mine is the fourth one along. Could you do this in silence and then as Lt. Cherry suggested, please do not speak of this ever again?' She stared up to where the shadowy head was, and was surprised when he placed a hand upon her shoulder, gently this time.

'You are not stupid, for you see the error you made clearly enough. I am pleased to have met such a level headed female instead of a feather brained, pretty bird. Will you be at the dinner tomorrow?' She did not answer because both heard someone approaching along the pathway. In one confident movement he swept his greatcoat around her and nestled her to him in the shadows. The warmth of his body contrasted to the cold of the night air. As soon as the gentleman passed by he unwrapped her again and walked with her further into the darkness of the alley.

'Listen to me please, Miss Mary Mason,' he whispered to her.

'Molly, please. It is a name my family used for me.'

'Miss Molly Mason,' he pulled her gently to him, 'I will see you safely home then we shall be as strangers when we are introduced tomorrow. I apologise for scaring you but Cherry did think his future business establishment was being robbed.'

'His?' Molly repeated, rather surprised that the Lieutenant was eyeing up the future prospects so carefully.

'Well, if he takes on Juniper, half the business becomes his as the bride-price so to speak. Did you not know?' She could hear the mirth in his voice.

'Why no, I presumed he was not just taking her on for the business. I thought it was a love match.' Molly did not think to hold her true thoughts back, so surprised was she that Cecily was prepared to go to such lengths to buy a husband of rank for her daughter. Molly wondered if even Juniper knew of it.

'You are quite lovely, miss. Do you also dream of love and heroes?' His voice was filled with more than a hint of undisguised sarcasm.

'No, sir. I dream of my own future. Not one saddled to a man!' Her voice had risen slightly and for a moment a lamp light brightened the alley as it was raised to a window. They huddled into the shadow behind a fence until the light was extinguished once more.

'I'm delighted to hear it. Fanciful dreams are easily shattered and their dreamers broken. You keep that level head and you shall not be misled. Now I believe this is your home. I shall wait until you are safely within before I go back to the inn.'

She stepped past him but his arm reached out and caught a gentle hold of her. 'Miss, you will not tell the girl about the arrangement, if she truly does not know the truth of the her marriage betrothal?'

'No . . . that I will not, but ask your friend to be kind to her because she will break if he is not.' She looked at him. In the half light she could not see him clearly; she stepped nearer to him so that she could see his eyes. 'He will be good to her, won't he?'

'I shall ask him to. I believe he is fond of her.' Molly could tell that his words were said in earnest but wondered why she should trust this stranger. Perhaps she was not thinking quite straight again. Then he did the most extraordinary thing. He leaned forwards and gently kissed her on her forehead. She was taken by his nerve; the experience was not at all unpleasant but presumptuous in the extreme. She backed away, turned and ran to the door of the house slipping in via the servants' entrance. With the door shut firmly behind her she breathed deeply and shook out the rolled up coat.

Once she found she could breathe easily again she ran up to her bed chamber and hung the coat behind her door. She looked out onto the alley but could see nothing but dark shadows. It gave her a sense of peace because anyone who had glanced at them would have seen only dark intangible shapes also. She touched her forehead lightly with her fingers and leaned against the window seat. A stolen kiss, her first, but who was the man? She would have to wait until dinner the following day before she found out his name. Her thoughts centred once more on tomorrow and her two existing appointments. It promised to be a day of mysteries and surprises.

She looked at the bed and her nightdress which had been laid across it ready for her. When her bedroom door was opened wide she gasped.

'Not ready yet?' Cecily asked. She was standing just inside the room.

'Ready, ma'am, for what?' she asked innocently. She could see the coat hung on the hook behind Cecily.

'For bed of course. What else? One of the servants thought she saw a man in the shadows in the alley. Did you?' Cecily asked her, watching as if she was unsure what had been happening, yet sensing something had.

'No, I was watching the moon. It is nearly full and quite beautiful, look . . . ' Molly pointed to the moon and the stars beyond.

Cecily took a step back into the doorway, fortunately not turning around and seeing the coat. 'Daydreaming! Always daydreaming! Change and go to bed. Take care, Mary Mason, not to cross me. You would regret it for a very long time if you ever did. Goodnight, my dear. Sweet dreams.' She left.

Molly stared at the door for a few moments before sinking onto the window seat, considering Cecily's threat very seriously.

5

Molly had a fitful night. Her mind felt as though it was trapped like a grain on a quern, being constantly turned round and round; each idea being pounded and ground down by the next. Sometimes she felt she was trying to be God-like, controlling the memories of recent events, back and fore in time. Even rearranging what had actually happened and how she had acted. Yet still she could not find any peace. Cecily had succeeded in unnerving her but, more than that, it was the stranger who had really disturbed her in some exciting yet dangerous way. She had liked him, she knew that too well. However, she did not like knowing that he had entered her life and taken control of both her situation and, for a moment in the shadows, even her. It would not happen again, of that she was determined, for no man was going to take the upper hand in her affairs or take control of her life.

However, one man could strongly influence it. That man was the mysterious Mr Gubbins. Molly was anxious to have the business disclosed to her she arose and washed, set her hair and took of a light snack to break her fast, then dressed. Unusually for Molly, she paid particular detail to her outfit, making sure that she matched or contrasted every item or accessory. The aim was to appear to this man of business as a woman who was confident and more 'worldly' than she actually was. The sooner she could make her way to the bakery and into Alice's understanding company, the sooner she would be able to relax; well, until the hour arrived when she would have to face Lt. Cherry and his friend. The thought of seeing her own friend and telling her what had transpired the previous evening lightened her mood, because Alice was a worldly woman and she would guide her as to how to handle the interview with Mr Gubbins and, of course, the stranger at dinner time. Mind, he would be like a stranger to her because in the half light she had barely seen his features clearly, although she had liked what she had seen. Molly almost forgot that between these two engagements she had to return to the shop to be with Juniper before the carriage arrived. Her stomach fluttered a little as the constraints upon her time made her anxious. She did not want to openly cross her stepmother.

Molly was surprised at how easy it was to leave the house unnoticed. She half expected to be summoned to the shop by Cecily for removing the coat rather quickly. Yet, none came.

Molly entered the bakery and was ushered straight into Alice's cosy little parlour. Here, lace abounded in the form of napkins, chair covers, cushion covers and the like. Her mother had loved making it, in what spare time she had, and Alice had inherited the knack of creating small pieces which she lovingly displayed.

'Now, don't you look grand? Who would have thought that you were a young woman now?' She gave her a big hug and kissed her on her cheek. 'I've got a present for you, Molly . . . ' Alice held out a neatly tied little parcel.

Molly opened the carefully folded cloth that had been lovingly wrapped around a pair of delicately made gloves. 'They're beautiful, Alice, so fine.'

'Oh, now don't cry, lass. I want you to be happy this day.' Alice looked at Molly; her own eyes were filled with moisture.

'Sorry, Alice, it's just that I'm so confused and I've so much to tell you and sometimes it feels as if you're the only one who understands me or cares.' She hugged Alice back feeling rather foolish and young, for where had her resolve gone to be a new woman? Vanished, she supposed.

'Come on, you are stronger than that. You're just a bit over-excited. I made you a cake, special for the day and one of your favourite pies. So tell me what you are so keen to share with me?' Alice sat her down next to her by the fire.

Molly wasted no time at all in sharing the exciting evening she had experienced.

'You don't even know this man's name?' Alice asked.

'No, nor who he is. How am I to face him at the table?' Molly flushed slightly.

'With confidence, that's how. He could be a good man. Just because he kissed you, don't mean he's a monster, he took you safely home. But Molly, lass, don't give him a second chance or else you'll be ruined for life. Talk travels fast and some men brag. You shall look him straight in the eye and in so doing you will have his measure. You'll soon know if he is a gentleman by the way he behaves toward you.' Alice shook her head. 'Lass, what were you thinking of going out at night on your own? What if you'd been mugged, raped or they'd forced the key to the shop off you? You could have been murdered!'

The worry on Alice's face made Molly swallow and flush even deeper.

'I only thought how near it was and how then I would not have to go to the shop in the morning. I was really scared, Alice. Don't be angry with me.'

'I'm not angry with you, Molly, but you could have been hurt and that would never do.' Alice smiled at her. 'The town is growing and there are strangers here now, you must take care. Come with me now and let me show you your cake.'

She took Molly by the hand and led her back into the shop. It was at that moment that Cecily entered the bakery from the street. She, too, was dressed to perfection.

'Mrs Creswell, what brings me the honour of your presence in person on this fine day?' Alice asked.

'I have been looking for my dear daughter . . . stepdaughter, that is, as she so often reminds people. Mary vanished this morning and one of my delivery men informed me he had seen her enter the baker's shop.' She smiled at Molly and looked at the gloves that she was holding in her hands. 'They are so lovely. Do I have a competitor in the town?' She looked at Alice.

'I'll stick to my baking, bread and such, if you don't mind.' Alice stepped behind her counter.

'Mrs Arndale invited me as it is my birthday, ma'am.' Molly addressed Mrs Creswell but the woman was far too relaxed. She was up to something, as if she was playing with them.

'Oh that would explain it then.' She stared at Molly.

'Explain what?' Alice asked.

'Simply why my own stepdaughter forgot to mention she had arranged for the interview with a Mr Gubbins to take place in a baker's shop in Bottom Alley. For surely you would not wittingly choose to hide such an arrangement from me.' She tilted her head on one side. Behind her Alice glanced up at the ceiling in exasperation.

'It's Lower Lane, Mrs Creswell,' Alice corrected.

Cecily glanced over her shoulder at her, 'Sorry, you will have to excuse me for I don't venture into this part of town very often. I let my housemaids do that . . . and my own stepdaughter it would appear.'

Molly looked at Cecily. 'I arranged to meet here because the letter I was given was addressed to me and me alone. It did not seem to involve anyone else. So, in order that the issue cause no ill feeling or confusion I decided to meet in the safety of Mrs Arndale's establishment until I knew precisely what this Mr Gubbins was about. I thought it the most sensible thing to do.' Molly was impressed by her own explanation. It appeared to cast a shadow of doubt over Cecily's face.

'I suppose you thought it would be best to slip out in the dark and go to my shop without permission and remove the coat . . . that very night from my shop. You did not think very clearly, girl

. . . woman, for the people who turn out at night are dangerous and you were lucky not to be taken for a trollop or a thief. You also spoiled my surprise to you for I was intending to present you with it this morning as a birthday gift — a token of my love for you, dear. Instead, I find you huddled up here. What am I to think, Mary?' Cecily removed a handkerchief from her pocket and sniffed at it.

'Did this Mr Gubbins invite you, too?' Alice asked, and saw that she had hit the mark when she received Cecily's glare by return.

'Do I need inviting? I am her guardian, her protector and provider. Of course, I should be included.' Cecily looked back at Molly. 'We should not have any secrets from each other.'

'Nor should we,' Molly replied, seeing the look of horror cross Alice's face.

'Good, then I shall wait with you.' Cecily replaced her handkerchief.

'No, ma'am, that you will not. I will

explain what has been said to me once I have had time to think it through. It may be nothing or something of import, but it is intended for me. You will have to trust me, Mrs Creswell and I shall come to you later.' Molly could only describe Cecily's response as bewilderment. She wanted to threaten and demand but obviously had no idea what Mr Gubbins was about and therefore what her deceased husband had planned from beyond the grave. Molly realised until that was known, Cecily, did not dare demand anything.

'But I am a woman of business. I can advise you.' Cecily looked vexed; she was not a woman to be dismissed easily.

'I shall not commit to anything at this meeting. I merely want to listen. Please, Mrs Creswell, let me deal with this, and trust me.'

Cecily stepped towards her. 'I warned you last night when you lied to me . . . it was you who the servant saw. You went out. You risked your reputation and my good name, why . . . to get your hands on that coat. Take it with my blessing and be at my shop by twenty minutes to two. Do not play me for a fool or you will lose more than the coat on your back.' She almost spun around and walked towards the door at a pace. 'Good day, Mrs Arndale, and if I may give you a sound piece of advice,' she glanced at Alice, 'be careful who you choose as your friends.' She slammed the door behind her and Molly stared at Alice feeling rather shaken.

'Tea and cake?' Alice said brightly, and ushered her back into the parlour whilst Sally took her place at the counter, looking more than a little sheepish.

6

Cecily made her way across the cobbled lane and entered the tea rooms opposite. It was one that was losing favour with her clientele since the expansion of the town and therefore she had no wish to linger longer than necessary. The area was being left behind in terms of social standing, as if in a medieval haze, whilst High Lane acted like a magnet to a different sort or person, people with money and a renewed sense of style, like herself. She aimed to stay in this clique. Cecily thought of the common woman, the baker opposite, and smiled, for Herbert should not lower his sights and settle for an old pair of comfy slippers when he could have new, uniquely woven silk pumps. He needed to raise ambitions in life, as she had. He may be a fat oaf, Cecily thought, but he had passed his mid years and had a successful business, which made him, in her eyes, a very good prospect for a future husband.

Once inside the dark panelled building, she made her way up the warped narrow twisting stairs to the upper floor and seated herself in the window seat, from which she could watch anyone who came and went into the bakery. It was how she had first realised her ungrateful stepdaughter was a frequent visitor. Thank goodness, she told herself, she had had the foresight to pay the girl, Sally, to keep her informed of young Molly's comings and goings . . . and Herbert's of course. But now, she was no longer 'young Molly'. Cecily was intrigued when Sally had reported that she was to meet a man called Gubbins in the bakery of all places, when they had a fashionable newly built home in which to receive respectable visitors. What was he to her? She wondered what information he had that did not involve her directly. Of all of her husbands, Molly's father had been the most pleasant, even enjoyable, and the most intelligent. So what had he left his headstrong daughter? It guiled her that she had not foreseen that he may have left separate instruction for her. Once she had the young Lieutenant hooked to her own Juniper, then she would sort out Miss Molly; after all, she was only a naïve young lass, no match for her when she thought of the men she had hoodwinked and outwitted in her lifetime.

Mind, the young Lieutenant was a prize catch. His family may have fallen on harder times than once they enjoyed, yet, his contacts were still good and so was his name. He'd taken her offer for the bride-price, with enthusiasm — a half a share in her shop. So quickly did he agree, that she knew he needed the money, and that was fine, because now she had the measure of him. So long as he was the perfect husband to Juniper and left her alone most of the time whilst he fought his wars, she as her mother would care for her and help to bring up the children. She sipped her tea and smiled at the thought. Grandchildren, the word rang pleasantly in her mind. All would be well. He had his business in London to attend to once he finished fighting the French. She placed the cup back on the saucer, and added a note to her thoughts and plans, which was — if he survived. Life could be so cruel, she mused, but Juniper would have her mother to console and advise her, so, in any event, all would be well, so long as Juniper had her mama.

★   ★   ★

The stranger saw Cecily leave the bakery and enter the tea rooms opposite. From the corner of the alley he had patiently waited and watched. As he expected, she seated herself at a table where, like a hawk sighting its prey, she could see the baker's frontage opposite.

He, too, waited his time, and when there was only fifteen minutes to the hour of one o clock showing on his time piece he entered the tea rooms making straight for the upper floor.

Removing his hat and greatcoat he placed them on the hat stand just inside the room door and, looking every inch the gentleman in his day suit, boldly walked over to where Cecily was seated. The building was an old wooden frame house, built in the medieval years which leant precariously over the alley in front. The uneven floor creaked under his feet; it had stood for centuries so he presumed it would stand at least for another quarter of an hour longer. All the old buildings in this part of town had been labelled as 'lower' by the more fashionable who bought the new houses that were rapidly expanding the town. The more prosperous and expensive housing claimed the right to the prestige of being named 'higher' in their address.

Cecily was completely absorbed in

her vigil and did not pay any attention to him as he approached.

'Good morning, ma'am,' he said, and waited for her to realise that she was being addressed.

She looked up at him, a little unsure as to why he was standing in front of her. 'Good day, sir.' She glanced quickly back out of the window almost dismissively.

'Would I be correct in my assumption that you are Mrs Cecily Creswell?' His voice was clear and, as she looked quizzically up at him, he saw her taken slightly aback by his sudden appearance at her side. She had been absorbed in her watch and looked flustered by the interruption.

'Yes, sir, I am. Please be so good as to introduce yourself as you have me at a disadvantage.' She looked him up and down, and as she showed some approval of what she saw, her voice softened slightly from its initial terse response.

'I am a friend of Lt. Cherry's

acquaintance; he was good enough to invite me to join him for dinner with your good family this evening. I hope this will not inconvenience you at all?' Her features were very fine for a woman approaching her mid years. He noted her clear skin, sensual lips and distinctive eyes. She still had a head of auburn hair; he could see why men fell for her attentions.

He relaxed his manner, emanating a smile that usually he reserved for impressing females he wished to win over. This lady responded and he then knew he had her measure. Everything he had been told about Mrs Cecily Creswell was surely true; she was a woman who liked to have her own way and knew how, with men at least, he thought.

'Of course, if you are Lt. Cherry's friend then indeed you are welcome at my table. It will not inconvenience me at all.' She broadened the smile on her lips as she noticed the fine stitching of his cuffs, then added almost as an afterthought, 'But do you have a name or are we to address you merely as 'a friend of Lt. Cherry's? Have we met before, sir?' She glanced back at the baker's shop quickly, clearly having been distracted, and then stared up at his fine features.

'You must excuse my bad manners, Mrs Creswell. We have never met before.' He seated himself opposite.

'I am well aware of that because I never forget a face . . . Particularly a pretty one such as yours.' She tried to look slightly coy as she flirted with him.

He grinned at her and continued trying not to enjoy the moment too much because he must not let his feelings come between him and his goal. 'My thanks, ma'am, but I am relieved my colleagues have not heard me described as such. It is a great shame we did not meet a few years ago for I could then have been at the wedding and welcomed you into the family formally.'

He had her attention now and so he

relaxed slightly. 'You see, if the world had not been in such a mess we should have met. If not for the wars, we could have also grieved together. But fate is a cruel mistress is she not?' He leaned back in the chair opposite her and stared at her puzzled, pale blue eyes — a resemblance to ice, he thought ironically.

'You intrigue me, sir. Did you know my late husband?' she asked, and quickly stole another quick glance out of the window.

'Yes, but not your last one. Not Mr Mason, the shoe maker of some note. My condolences, Mrs Creswell or Mrs Mason, if we are to be accurate,' he said, and looked as sincere as he could manage. 'Ill fortune, in love at least, has dogged your heels. However, the one you still carry the name of, Mr Jeremy Creswell — your previous husband and a truly good man.' He did not have to mock sincerity as he spoke the last sentence.

'Yes . . . he was.' She stared intently

at him, puzzled, unnerved, and now he had her total attention as she hungered to know how he knew her namesake. 'Who are you, sir? I feel you are toying with me. Please speak out and end this cruel taunt.'

'No, you misunderstand me. I merely wished to lessen the shock that my news will surely bring you; for I could not possibly announce myself to you at your party without having first explained my presence. You see, it was by sheer chance that I was rescued by Lt. Cherry's unit and, as a result, our friendship grew. He told me he also was returning to England to announce his betrothal to Miss Juniper Creswell — a name she was given to stay the same as her dear mama, because her birth name of . . .'

'The reason was simple, we had a business. It made life too complicated if we carried different surnames.'

'Especially a French one,' he added.

'It was only the name that was French! Now please explain yourself for you have obviously asked Mr Cherry a deal of questions about my family. Why, sir?'

'I would have been at the wedding, but I was lost, presumed captured or dead behind enemy lines,' he explained and then saw her face pale as she realised the truth of it. She had also presumed him to be dead.

'I am, as you have correctly presumed, Mr Julian Creswell. My father must have found such solace in the arms of such a charming lady and at such a vulnerable time in his life as losing his only son, not three years after his wife, my mother, was taken from him.' He saw her eyes harden at the last comment. 'However, I am returned. I was injured, but am now free to retire from service and resume my father's business interests and control my inheritance here in England. So here I am. But I understand you have invested some of it wisely in a business right here and the rest we shall discuss when my solicitor arrives tomorrow.'

Her face paled further and her hand shook slightly.

'I'm sorry to break this news to you so abruptly, there did not seem to be a more gentle way, or a more convenient time. Lt. Cherry is excited at the prospect of a family reunion, but of course I did not want to spoil his enthusiasm with complications . . . and I realise there may well be complications.' He placed his hand on hers but she withdrew it quickly, looking at him as if he was the epitome of evil personified

'You can prove this?' she asked incredulously.

'Oh, definitely! I am no trickster, ma'am. Please believe me, this circumstance is as big a shock for me as for you. I have learned that on my return, instead of a father to greet me, I find he died not knowing that I lived and that in the long months that I was incarcerated took a new wife and widowed her. So my previous life is now no more.'

He could see clearly that the time of Mr Gubbins arrival was passing Cecily by as eyes were fixed upon his face, seeking a likeness perhaps, in his features, to her husband. 'Don't worry, Mrs Mason, for I understand it is difficult for a lady to exist in this world on her own. I am only sorry that your next husband died also. Was he your third husband? You have been seriously aggrieved these last few years.'

She reached out a hand and touched his. 'You poor thing, how cruel life's twists can be. You have had your world turned upside down and all in the time you chose to defend your king and country.'

'Thank you for being so understanding. Now, may I suggest that we set all this aside and compose ourselves for this evening's celebration; for is it not a divine coincidence that your lovely daughter is to wed my friend Lt. Cherry and together will share in my inheritance, and that you shall be so happy at their good fortune, for I wish them nothing but happiness.' He removed his hand from hers.

Cecily stood up, clearly gathering her wits as she strove to regain control of the events that had unfolded before her. 'Sir, your arrival is a shock to me . . . as well as a delight. We shall indeed talk in greater depth of family matters. However, you are quite correct we must put my daughter's happiness first. She glanced quickly out of the window then at the clock on the wall and sighed, knowing she had let the moment go and was no nearer understanding what this Mr Gubbins was about. She hoped the girl, Sally, would be worth her coin and tell her all she hears accurately. But the girl was stupid, so she held out little hope for that.

Julian stood up also, his tall frame slightly stooped as he avoided a low beam. 'May I escort you back to your home? You look a little pale, ma'am.'

'Please don't bother yourself about me, Julian. You shall be welcome in my home for dinner and if you need somewhere to stay you may of course use one of our rooms. In fact, my dear boy, don't worry yourself about my constitution at all, it is, I assure you quite strong. Life, as you so rightly pointed out to me, has dealt me a number of cruel blows. But your presence here shall add to our celebration, Julian.' She smiled at him sweetly before leaving.

He watched her cross the road from the window and admired her nerve, but hated every bone in her body; and that was rare for him, for even in the heat of battle he did not hate the men he fought; he had merely done his duty as they had done theirs. But this was a very different kind of battle. This involved wits, and he had found a worthy adversary — one who had already outwitted his own father.

7

Molly was very shaken by Cecily's arrival. She was nervous enough about seeing this strange man without dealing with the guilt of knowing their clandestine meeting had been discovered by her stepmother.

'Calm yourself, lass.' Alice ushered her back into the parlour. 'I should have got that bell fixed on me door. It's supposed to jingle when anyone enters.'

'How on earth did that woman know that I was meeting him here?' She looked at Alice. 'I've been so careful not to give anything away. It is as though she had someone following me.' Molly sighed. She rarely felt defeated but this time she did.

'Well, that she hasn't . . . unless . . . ' Alice glanced to the bakery door. She lowered her voice to a whisper. 'I've been blind. Under me own nose, in me

own house! I've fed her and given her work. I'll skin that girl, the little bitch ... a leach that's what she is ... '
Alice's face flushed crimson.

Realising that Alice meant the person who had betrayed them both, was none other than young Sally, Molly grabbed Alice's arm and stopped her from rushing back out of the room.

'Don't confront her. If we know she is Cecily's spy we may be able to use her to our own advantage. Right now, though, I need privacy. Send her on an errand that will take her the best part of the afternoon to complete, Alice,' Molly almost begged her.

Alice nodded. 'Aye, I'll do that. Leave it to me. She'll have no idea who's been and went. It'll give me time to calm down too and lose this notion I have to beat the stupid fool senseless. You get yourself ready, lass. Have that tea and calm yourself down also. I'll join you in a moment.' She winked at Molly with her usual good humour and then in her normal voice, that would carry through into the bakery should anyone be listening to their conversation, she said brightly, 'Molly! Here I am so wrapped up in you and your birthday that I forgot about me flour order. Never mind, I'll send young Sally to the mill post haste, as it were.' She walked over to the door and shouted, 'Sally!'

Quick as a flash Sally was in the doorway of the parlour. 'Yes, Mrs Arndale?'

Alice smiled, as she normally would have at the young girl, but cast a knowing glance over to Molly. 'There you are. I need you to take this order to the mill. It shouldn't take you more than an hour or two to walk there and back.' Alice produced a piece of paper from her pocket.

Sally looked a little pale. 'But . . . there's the shop to watch . . . ' she looked from one woman to the other, 'And you've got a guest, Mrs Arndale — shouldn't I wait till the lady's gone, ma'am?'

'Why no, I'm capable of looking after

my own shop, girl. What ideas you have. Now go on and don't dawdle. No stopping to chat along the way. The sooner you go the sooner you'll be back and then I dare say you can have one of me small pies. Now hop to.' Alice shooed the girl out giving her no call for more excuses.

Molly waited a few moments until Alice returned. 'I thought you had gone with her,' she said as Mrs Arndale entered the room.

'You never guess who I just saw leave the tea rooms walking like there was a ghost behind her?' Alice was quite excited.

'What sort of a walk is that, Alice?' Molly asked, grinning at her friend for the first time on what was proving to be a most intriguing day.

'A bloody fast one, lass, and with no looking back,' Alice added quickly, and seated herself opposite her friend.

'Well who?' Molly smiled.

'Cecily Creswell, that's who, so why do you think she was leaving her perch?' Alice continued.

'Someone scared her off it? A ghost perhaps?' Molly suggested, but her smile had gone.

'You are not a million miles from the truth, miss,' The deep voice who answered them made both women stand up in surprise. Instantly, the stranger apologised. 'I'm sorry but there was no one in the shop and it is now past one o' Clock. I did not mean to eavesdrop or scare either of you ladies.'

Molly stared at the stranger who she had met the previous night. He was more handsome in the daylight than she had given him credit. He had a rough, worldly look to him. Not the look of the dandy or the pampered gentleman. Yet she thought he appeared to be well bred. He stood straight and his voice spoke in a confident manner.'

'I really will have to get that bell fixed. Excuse me, Mr Gubbins, I presume, whilst I lock the door before the whole town converges on me little shop.' She stepped out of the room, glancing at a speechless Molly as she passed her. 'I'll be back in a second,' she added, much to Molly's relief.

Molly had wanted to appear to be a more mature woman for this meeting, adding sophistication to her carefully chosen apparel, yet here she was facing the man who had found her walking the street at night. How cruel, Molly thought, fate could be.

* * *

Sally ran straight from the lower town to the back of the High Lane shops. Frantically, she knocked on the back door of Mrs Creswell's shop. Eventually, it was Juniper who answered it as the girls were busy helping her mama complete a fitting. Her mother had left in a happy mood and returned in a frightful one.

'What on earth are you playing at, girl? Are you trying to bring down the building,' Juniper snapped indignantly.

'I need to tell your mother that they've sent me out on an errand and I won't be there to . . . to hear anything that's said, miss.'

Juniper frowned. 'She will not be pleased. Do they suspect you? Have you disclosed your evil nature to them?' Juniper almost glared at the frightened young girl.

'No . . . no . . . it's just the order hasn't been sent to the mill, and I have to take it.'

'Well, I'll tell my mother. But she will not be pleased!' Juniper said sharply.

'My . . . coin . . . will I still get it? I came as she asked,' the girl added hopefully.

'Insolent wretch!' Juniper snapped, she close the door as she went back into the shop.

Sally looked at it and uttered one word, 'Bitch!'

It took her by surprise when the door promptly opened again and a hand swiped her across the cheek. 'Don't dare to insult your betters!' Juniper

76

slammed the door shut leaving a crestfallen Sally to run to the mill. She would have to run to try to make up for lost time, with a flea in her ear, a sting on her face and hatred in her heart.

* * *

Alice returned before a word had been spoken between Molly and the stranger. They both seemed lost in their own thoughts as they watched each other, intrigued yet wary.

'Who are you, sir? Mr Gubbins or whom?' Molly found the confidence to talk once Alice was with them again.

'I apologise, Miss Mason, for I am not he. In truth, he does not exist, but I needed to lure you away from your family.' He looked at Alice almost apologetically. 'I sincerely apologise for this subterfuge.'

'They are not 'my' true family, sir. They are my step family — by marriage only. So who are you and what sick game do you play raising my hopes that my father had kept something special back for me?' Molly saw his expression change and she realised this man had not meant to taunt her deliberately or cause her pain.

'I know all about Mrs Cecily Creswell, or as much as I need to. I also know that your father and her previous husband were good friends. He left this packet with my father's solicitors in safe keeping for you.' He handed her a parcel neatly tied in ribbon and sealed with wax. It looked quite important — official even. Molly took it and looked at the stranger.

'I believe that it contains some personal effects of your mother's, which he wished to be handed down to you on your twenty-first birthday.'

'Why did he not leave it with Mrs Cresswell, his wife?' Molly asked.

'Simply because he did not trust her to deliver it; in fact, Miss Mason, he did not trust her at all.'

'Who are you, sir?' Molly asked, determined to find out who the man who had stolen a kiss from her the previous night was. Why was he standing before her now, telling her all this?

He looked at her. 'Miss, my name is Julian Creswell and I need to talk to you, in the strictest confidence.'

8

Molly considered him warily then glanced to Alice to see if she could read the woman's reaction to this surprise introduction. 'You are her son?' Alice asked, obviously taken aback.

'No more than Miss Mason is her daughter, which is why if you are the person that my father and yours described in their letters to each other, then you are also possibly in danger from her.' He was staring at Molly. 'I don't want to scare you, but I need to speak the truth as I perceive it.'

'Please, Mr Creswell, sit down and let us talk openly,' Alice Arndale spoke and patted the chair next to the small table adjacent to her own.

Molly studied at the package in her hands, not knowing what to do with it. Should she open it in front of the stranger or just listen to what he said?

This whole circumstance was both confusing and worrying. She had never trusted Cecily but how serious was the danger she was in?

'Pardon me, ma'am, for asking, but who are you to Miss Mason, other than the owner of the bakery?' He sat down as requested; his manner was sincere rather than offensive.

'She is my friend and confidant. Anything you wish to say has to be said in front of Mrs Arndale and I would appreciate it if you would not prevaricate as I am expected to be at the shop in forty minutes,' Molly said.

'Then I shall be brief. I was assumed to be dead, after being lost in Spain behind enemy lines. I had actually been taken prisoner, and was injured. However, I survived and in time, more than a year later, I was freed. My father had been sent a message saying that I was presumed dead. He met Cecily at this time, or should I say that she contrived to meet him. She had read the letter. I understand she dropped in so was actually in our home at the time, enquiring as to a housekeeper's position; her fortunes from her first husband's estate were, I have discovered, dwindling fast. She needed to remarry in order to rear her daughter as she wished and to improve their lot. She turned her charms and affections on a lonely, bereaved man. A year passed and the presumption of my demise was confirmed as correct. He married and lived for a further nine months to regret it. During this time he had written to your father and confessed to his old friend that all was not sweet in either the marital bed, or in the marriage itself. He had come to feel lonelier than ever.'

Molly watched as he paused for a moment and both women realised that raw emotion was welling up inside him. They exchanged empathetic looks as both could feel the hurt emanating from this strong, yet vulnerable, man.

'You must excuse me, ladies. I must be softening since my return to

England. If I had behaved in such a manner in Spain I should never have survived. Not exactly what you would expect from a soldier is it?' He forced a smile.

'It is no more than I would expect from a loving son, who has been robbed of his father, though,' Molly replied, stifling her own pains as she spoke.

'You see the situation correctly, miss. I was very close to Father, and all that has happened has become a huge shock to me also.' He tilted his head back, breathed in deeply and restored his composure. 'My apologies to you both.'

'We understand, lad. You take your time. You're welcome to stay here if you need a roof over your head.' Alice spoke up.

'I've accepted Cecily's offer for that already.'

Alice raised a questioning eyebrow. 'Is that wise, if you are here to protect Miss Mason?'

'Is it possible you can bear to be in the same room as her?' Molly asked.

'Yes. I do not want Cecily to know that I suspect her part in my father's death, or in that of your own father. I aim to play her at her own game and to find her out. You see, I think she poisoned them somehow, but I cannot prove it. However, I would like to be there to watch over you also, Miss Mason. The letters I found led me to believe that your father was trying to protect your future and there may be something of import within that parcel. I would not let Cecily see it, but I would be honoured and relieved if you would share the secret with me. Either way, I would offer you a safe haven away from that woman. The short answer is I need to find out the truth, but I may be wrong. She might just be an evil woman who wears her husbands down. Will you help to solve this interminable puzzle?'

'I had in fact made plans to move out. I was thinking of taking up a room here and helping Mrs Arndale as her apprentice,' Molly explained. 'It is just that when you . . . Mr Gubbins that is, sent word to me, I had hoped that I would be able afford to free myself of Cecily for good.'

'It's a fanciful notion, but she is welcome here, but Creswell — sorry, lad, I should say Mrs Creswell — would not be best pleased.' Alice folded her arms across her apron. 'Open the packet, lass, and let's see what's in there and that will help you know what to do,' Alice advised her.

'Perhaps we should leave Molly alone for a few moments.' Julian began to stand but Molly placed a hand on his leg to stop him.

'No. Stay. I think we both need to share our resources. I, too, would like to read the letters of which you spoke. I have little enough of my father as it is.' She could see the relief in his deep brown eyes and she knew instantly that this was the right decision. She had, though, left her hand on his knee and, as he sat back down, he carefully placed his over it.

Alice stood up. 'If you'll excuse me a minute I've bread to check up on and I think we all need a cup of tea.' She walked over to the door and the two hands quickly separated.

Molly was about to open the packet when her eyes found his. 'Tell me one thing, sir. In the alley, did you know who I was from the start?'

She saw a humorous smile cross his face. 'I confess from all that I have heard and read of you, it did enter my mind who you were. However, I needed Cherry to confirm it and you were out at a dangerous hour.'

'So why did you presume to kiss me?' She tried to sound vexed but her curiosity came to the fore.

'Because I acted on impulse and I make no apology for it. I'd gladly do it again, but would rather it was freely given rather than taken as a thief . . . '

'In the night,' Molly whispered.

'Exactly! Did I offend you?' he asked quietly. 'It was not my intention.'

'Look, here we are chatting and time

marches on.' She opened the paper and lifted out an embroidered pouch avoiding answering his question, because offended was far from how she had felt. Within the package she found her mother's precious rings, her necklace, a string of small pearls and a mother of pearl comb and mirror. She had not seen them for years, presuming that Cecily had lied when she had denied selling them. Placing them individually and carefully back within the pouch, she then found a key. Under the key was a leather wallet containing fifty pounds in coin and note. This was more money than she had ever seen. She glanced up at Julian who she was amused to see was deliberately looking elsewhere.

'What a strange mixture of a man you are. One minute bold as brass and kissing me, the next the perfect gentleman and looking away lest you pry uninvited. Look, see what is here. I have some means of my own at last!' Molly was clearly excited.

'It is a nice sum, miss, but it will not

pay for your independence.' He picked up the key. 'What is this for?'

'I don't know. I recognise it, for father frequently carried it under his shirt. He said he kept it close to his heart. It used to be on a narrow chain.' Molly lifted the wallet up but there was no separate letter.

'May I?' Julian gestured to the wallet.

'Yes, of course.' She held it out to him.

He turned it over and over in his hands and then removed the money inside, handing it to Molly. His fingers felt inside each division until he retrieved a fine piece of vellum from between an inner pocket. 'This may give you the information that you seek.'

Molly opened it and read the short note. She could not help herself flush with emotion. Water-filled eyes glanced up at Julian. 'I miss him so,' she said simply.

He placed an arm around her and drew her to him. They said nothing, as there was nothing to say. But two kindred spirits found a few moments of comfort in each other's arms.

The door opened behind them and a tray was placed on the table. Alice turned as if to speak to them but this time they did not separate, lost as they were in each other's comfort.

'I'll just go check me bread . . . again,' Alice muttered before shutting the door behind her.

9

Molly read the note but folded the piece of fine vellum carefully again and placed it with the jewellery inside the embroidered pouch. 'We must have the tea quickly or Alice will be offended and I only have a quarter of an hour before the coach is due at the shop to take me to a previously made appointment. I think it is best if I act as normal and do not raise Cecily's suspicions.' She was relieved when Alice returned as they poured the liquid out of the pot. 'I know the woman is hard and selfish but do you really think she is capable of murder?'

The moments they had hugged each other had been like a tonic to Molly. She had felt warmth and protection of another human being and the stirrings of far deeper emotions. It was when these emotions threatened to creep to the fore that they both sat up straight and, not really knowing what to say to each other, had returned their attentions to the items in the packet. The note, though, she had read herself, but had not shared the contents with Julian.

'I don't honestly know. If she hasn't aided them to an early grave then both she and they have had very bad luck. I just feel totally uneasy about the convenience of it all for her. Besides, I have to sort out what is left of my inheritance. I shall now take control of any finances I can prove have come from my father's estate, or the residue. Was your father a wealthy man?'

'He never lacked for money. He had two apprentices and another workshop at the far end of town. It mainly supplied the farmers. I know that Cecily was disappointed when the will was read, though, because she had hoped to be able to employ someone to run the shop for her so she could be a 'proper' lady of the town. There was not sufficient funds for a house, staff and a manager for the shop.' Alice stared into the fire's flames; they rose and fell, burned and died and then were gone, like life itself burned out.

'Then I think there is possibly more there . . . somewhere waiting for you to find or collect. The problem you will face is where and how to get at it.' Julian patted her knee. 'I hope you like a mystery.'

She met his stare and smiled. 'I think I am looking straight at one right now.' He removed his hand and laughed at her comments. 'Alice, I shall take the jewellery with me for that will explain the mystery visit of Mr Gubbins to Cecily. I shall also take a few coins from the wallet but would ask you to protect my other monies? I shall decide what to do with it when I have had time to think this all through.' She smiled as the woman took the wallet and placed it in her safe behind a cupboard door.

'What of the key and the note, Molly?' Julian asked.

'The key I would ask you to keep

with you at all times.'

'Do you think that is wise?' asked Alice boldly, for it was obvious that she did not.

Molly nodded. 'Yes, I do, Alice. I shall discuss the importance of it with you, Julian, after dinner tonight when Juniper and Cecily are asleep in bed.' Molly thought carefully for a moment. 'I shall come to your room, no one would expect that of me.'

'Too right they wouldn't! You'll do no such thing, lass!' Alice exclaimed. 'Mister Creswell, you seem in earnest but this naïve little fool does not know what she is saying. She cannot go traipsing along landings to a man's room at night — or any other time of day for that matter!' Alice was all of a fluster.

'Alice! How could you say such a thing? I was only meaning that it would not be expected of me and therefore would be the safest place for us to meet,' Molly exclaimed, but Alice glanced up at the ceiling in mock despair.

'Safe? A man's bed chamber is safe? How will you survive with a reputation worth having if you go through life acting on such careless impulses?'

It was Julian who interrupted before Alice vented what she was truly thinking about Molly's innocent suggestion.

'Ladies, please. I also think it would be entirely wrong. I will not allow you to risk your reputation in such a cavalier manner. It would be a rather rash act. Alice has made her objection because she obviously cares a great deal about your welfare and therefore she is quite correct to. I shall guard the key safely, if that is what you wish, and tomorrow we shall find time to talk once more. However, I would like to know what of the note, Molly?' He looked at her. 'What is it?'

'It was a personal message from my father. I shall keep it safe. Cecily is bound to rummage through my belongings. She will not think anything of my receiving jewellery and a note on such a day as this, but the key and money are items that I do not wish her to know about. Also, she must not know that we are acquainted. So when we are introduced this evening, Mr Creswell, it will be as strangers, unless Lt. Cherry speaks of last night's encounter to Miss Juniper.'

'That he will not, Molly. He has no wish to have been seen in the town before his arrival to your home this evening. He was visiting an old friend, shall we say.' He glanced at Alice a little sheepishly.

'If she was an old friend of his who resides at the inn I can imagine who it was.' Alice shook her head. 'Poor Juniper,' she muttered quietly.

Molly looked bemused, but was conscious of time going quickly by. 'Now I must go back before I create more tension between myself and Cecily. Good day, sir.'

He stood up and bowed slightly to her as she replaced her gloves.

'Thank you, Alice, for the gift, the

cake and your discreet hospitality.'

'That's all right. I enjoyed making and providing them.' Alice let Molly kiss her cheek and then watched her walk to the door. Julian, who was standing next to Alice, turned to bid her good day also.

'Sir, you will stay a moment. I would like a word with you and I don't want you leaving through the front door and be seen following Molly.'

Molly glanced back at Alice before she left and saw Julian wink at her discreetly as he seated himself next to Alice once again. Molly had a feeling she was about to lecture him on what was good manners, his duty to protect her and propriety. She smiled broadly to herself and with her mother's few precious belongings in her hand made her way back to Creswell's dressmakers extraordinaire.

10

Molly made quick progress toward the shop. She could see the coach was already approaching. With her mother's jewellery in her hand and wearing her new coat, she felt like a different more confident person. Knowing that she had some money of her own also helped to boost her confidence — Cecily had not received it all. It felt to her as though both her parents had given her a special gift to mark her day. She refused to let maudlin thoughts creep in to her mind, wishing that they were both still there with her. They were not and never could be again. She looked at the embroidered pouch and felt a warm feeling inside of her. It meant a lot to have these few precious things. She thought of Julian, despite the chill of his message and the fear of Cecily that it had deepened within her; his touch had brought a very different kind of warmth to her body. She composed herself ready to face Cecily's questioning.

Opening the door wide, she saw that Juniper was already standing with her own green velvet coat on. She had had to have a new one, of course, even though it was not her birthday; she could never be outdone by Molly.

'Our wanderer has decided to return, Juniper. Does this mean that you will not be setting up home on your own yet, dear Mary?' Cecily's wit was sharp as a knife.

'Why, no, of course I will not. Look, ma'am, I have been left my mother's jewellery. It had been kept safely for me, to mark my birthday. Isn't it a fine thought?' She smiled from one to another and watched as both fumbled her few precious mementos.

'Fine gesture, just don't wear them in public, girl, they are so dated,' Cecily said, and absently dropped them back into the bag. Then her eyes caught sight of the folded piece of vellum. She pulled it free and opened it out so that Juniper could see it also.

Juniper read the words aloud . . .

My dearest Molly,

I'm sorry that I cannot be with you in person but you see my health is fading as the years pass me by. I wanted you to have these few things of your dear Mama's so that you could treasure them as I have.

We loved you dearly when we were together and still do. I want you to remember, Molly, that special place we held dear . . . in our hearts, where I said you could always find something of me when you need my help, and you will always find the truth of my words remembered.

With all my love,
Your Father.

'And what is this place of which he speaks?' Cecily asked, her eyes narrowing as if an important secret was to be divulged.

'Inside my heart, of course, memories of words of wisdom which he spoke to me,' Molly answered, and looked from one unimpressed face to the other. 'Father always believed we kept a part of our loved ones in our heart when they left this earth.'

'How quaint,' Juniper said, insincerely.

Molly replaced the note and Cecily had already turned her back to her to move back to her business. 'Don't be late, girls. Now, Molly can focus on preparing herself to be civil at the dinner table tonight for our guests.' Cecily looked genuinely pleased at the thought.

'Guests?' Molly repeated. 'I thought the lieutenant was arriving alone.' Molly played her innocent part to perfection.

'He has sent word that he is bringing a friend with him. A distant relative of mine whom he had chance to rescue in Spain,' she said sweetly, and smiled at a positively glowing Juniper. 'So, you shall have a young man to entertain also. It is proving to be a very promising day for you, girl.'

'The coach is here, Mama,' Juniper said, excitedly.

'Go and have a lovely time telling that boring child about your young Lt., Juniper.' Cecily opened the door for her daughter then looked at Molly. 'Indeed, it is a shame your father had not left you more, but at least now you might appreciate how fortunate you are to live in such a fine house and wear elegant clothes on your back, girl.'

'But I do, ma'am.' Molly looked straight into the icy blue eyes.

'Never, ever, dare to hide a rendez-vous from me again or you shall lose both! Do you understand, miss? My charity can only be pushed so far.'

Molly looked down, as if shame-faced. 'I'm sorry, ma'am, I did not think it through properly,' Molly said quietly. 'I was so excited that someone wanted to see me about my father.'

'In future, leave the thinking to me.

You just concentrate on showing my clothes off to their best advantage.' Cecily glared at her and Molly nodded agreement. The woman smiled broadly, her victory regarded as complete. 'Good! Enjoy your visit.'

The door was shut behind her and Molly decided she would, because the only person who knew of her father's special place was Molly herself. But she also needed Julian to help her, and that was why he had the key in safe keeping. She would have to be patient, but then that was a virtue she had learned, thanks to the taunts of Cecily.

★   ★   ★

The journey started in silence. Juniper sat opposite Molly, looking out of the window at first as they left the town. They had to pass through lower lane to join onto the moor road.

Juniper laughed and looked at Molly. 'So your fortune is incomplete; merely a few old pieces of metal.'

Molly was quite surprised by the bitterness in the girl's voice. She was usually quiet; lately, though, as her betrothal drew near though she had been more outspoken.

'I am delighted with my mother's belongings. Wouldn't you be if anything had happened to your own mama?' Molly saw her face change as her lips set in a firm line.

'How dare you talk about Mama in that way. Do you wish her dead?' She was leaning forward as she spoke, almost accusingly.

'Of course not. I was just trying to make you see how important they are to me. I was as close to my mother as you are to yours. You should be able to understand that, surely.' Molly stared at her and the girl sat back.

'Yes, I suppose,' she said casually as she looked out of the window. 'I am just a little excited about meeting Archibald again. He is such a hero. Mama said he rescued her relation — Creswell's own son — from the French in Spain, all by himself. I bet he looks older and worldlier now. He may even have been injured. Who knows what scars he carries? The poor man must be so brave.' Juniper's eyes seemed to be lost in a private haze as she watched the moor stretch out before them.

'What do you know of the other man?' Molly asked.

'I know he is older than Archibald and obviously more of a fool or else how would he have been caught in the first place? You should make a play for him, though. Time is not on your side. If you do not wish to be an old maid then set your cap at him. He may even find your connections make you an attractive proposition.'

'I shall see what the gentleman is like first. I have no wish to 'connect' with anyone who is not of an admirable character.' Molly saw Juniper smile.

'Don't you understand anything? You want a man who can provide for your comforts. It matters not what his character is, because if you don't like him you can use your guile to send him away from you whilst enjoying his home and trappings. Otherwise, you shall be so picky that no one will take you and you will be destined to be an old maid. No one wants that!'

Molly did not answer. Instead, she sat in silence wondering just how calculative and cold Juniper really was. She certainly was a credit to Cecily's upbringing.

11

The afternoon had dragged on relentlessly. Juniper had regaled the whole tale of her hero, Archibald, and how he had rescued her stepbrother as if guided by an angel, bringing him home to be with her mama. She did not stop there, she described how selflessly he was suffering the ordeal of travelling overnight across high seas and then to continue the long journey up country just to be with her for dinner that very night. There had been no escape for Molly and her friend to spend some time on their own, so Molly had withdrawn into her thoughts whilst the more impressionable girl listened to Juniper, hanging on her every word — or manufactured lie.

Molly's own thoughts returned over and over to her father and the place they had called their own. How soon she would be able to return there she knew not, but the answer to her escape from Cecily's grip surely lay in some sort of box hidden in that lonely place. That took her thoughts down a totally different track concerning Julian. She lingered on them, wondering what Juniper's reaction would be when she saw her 'hero', looking rather rougher than he had the last time she had seen him as the youth who had gone to war, full of ideals and heroic notions, next to the more mature stature of the handsome Julian. True, he did not look like he would be comfortable with the idle gossip of the assembly rooms. Rather she assumed he would be more at home on horseback riding across open country, but he had a strength and energy about him that Lt. Cherry certainly lacked.

They returned to the carriage and the short journey back home promptly on the hour as Cecily had insisted.

Juniper sighed as the coach pulled away. 'I think Mama is planning a spring wedding for me. I cannot wait. I so want to be a proper 'woman',' She smiled at Molly.

'You shock me, Juniper.' Molly smiled back at her.

'Well I ought not. Surely, you must wonder what it is like to be held in the arms of a man, don't you?' Juniper watched her, and Molly realised she was trying to pry.

Molly just shrugged her shoulders.

'Well I do, and soon I shall find out. Mama said it can be quite enjoyable, depending on the man.' She looked so content with herself. But Molly found herself wondering which man had managed to satisfy Cecily Creswell.

'I've already chosen the dresses. Mine is divine. You will be my bridesmaid — or is it maid of honour? I'm not sure if age is taken into account. Mama will, though. You will wear a more cheerful countenance than you did today, I sincerely hope. Are you ailing, or just disappointed that you were not left a small fortune by your father?' Juniper raised her head in a slightly aloof manner.

'Neither, I merely thought you had more to say, so I decided to listen instead. One learns so much more by listening, Juniper, than by endlessly talking.' Molly looked at her, the cheeks flushed. The girl often tried to mimic her mother's acidic tongue but Molly could always outwit her as she simply was not quick enough with the retort.

'If we don't share what we learn then we are being truly selfish!' Juniper snapped back quickly.

'You are definitely not selfish then.' Molly saw a satisfied expression cross Juniper's face, so Molly gazed out of the window and enjoyed the view, tired of her companion's small talk.

★ ★ ★

'Archie, get up man!' Julian entered the room at the inn and drew back a heavy curtain. The light flooded into the room, showing the dust in the air from the fabric as it was moved. He pulled on the quilted bed cover revealing Archibald's bare chest and three arms. 'Sally,' Julian laughed, 'go on with you.' He tossed her a coin that she happily caught, stepped out of the bed as naked as the day she was born and pulled on her dress.

'Thank you, mister.' She smiled at Julian. 'I'll not tell Mrs Creswell that you was here. I swear I'll not tell that woman a thing again,' she said, 'unless you pay me to.' She smiled at the thought and winked.

'Good girl. You tell me what she asks you to do next, Sally, and that coin might turn into a silver or even a gold one. She doesn't respect you, like we do. She just uses you.' Julian nodded knowingly at her.

'Yeh, I know how much you respect me, don't you worry,' Sally replied and laughed again. 'But you pay better and besides, you're better looking than that bitch and the young miss. I hate 'em both.' Sally glanced at Julian's timepiece. 'Bloody hell, Mrs Arndale will be mad as hell. I'm real late!'

Archibald stretched over to the side table and gave her another coin. 'Tell her it was worth it.' He gave her one last kiss and the girl left them, happy and a little richer. She broke into a run as she went.

'Oh, Julian, can I really go through with this?' He stood up and walked over to the wash stand.

'Yes, you can, Cherry. Whatever I find out won't change things between you and your Juniper unless you wish it.' He leaned against a chair.

'I don't mind the girl; she is sweet and led astray by her mother. If I can break her away from the old bat then I am sure we will be happy. You can have your inheritance back; I'll sign the shop over to you as soon as we are wed. I don't need to steal from friends. You have lost enough already. Small world, isn't it, that our paths should cross so? However, I want to take Juniper back to London and then out to my father's cottage in Kent. I intend to go back to hop growing and the orchards. I'm sure that Juniper will love the country and the freedom it offers. But I shall not speak a word of it to her until we are married, for sure she will confide in Cecily. Besides, if your worst fears are true she will need somewhere to go away from the world to recover from the shock.' He dressed, then looked at Julian. 'Do you think it is wise to eat in her home? You know that this is a far-fetched notion. To accuse someone of cold blooded murder is worse than killing on a battlefield.'

'Yes, because we will carefully play along with her. She will not want to raise any further questions. She has too much to lose.' Julian was very thoughtful.

'What about the young woman, Molly Mason? Do you find her as you expected? Is she an innocent in all of this? Is she quick witted as her father described, or a strong natured harridan?' Archibald asked and smiled when his friend hesitated before answering.

'I find her well . . . very well.' Julian grinned.

'Can this be true that the great hero, the soldier of note, has found a soft spot,' Archibald teased. 'Are you becoming fond of a girl you have known for only a few hours? Love at first sight?' The man laughed.

'Do not forget that for this purpose it is you who is the hero. You rescued me from Spain . . . I am beholden to you,' Julian said quietly, ignoring his jibe.

'Yes, but it was you who broke us out of that prison and me who still has the nightmares about it.' Archibald looked down shame-faced. 'I wish they would go away, but it was the beatings, they . . . '

'They taunted you but you did not break under pressure. So let it go and do not do it now. No one need know what happened, Archie, the truth will die with us. So enjoy being a hero and I shall enjoy being indebted.' He patted Archibald on the shoulder. 'The nightmares will go. As you find happiness with your wife, you will forget all about the wars,' he glanced at the time, 'We must also dress or we shall be late, Lt. — and that would never do.'

'You just want to see your Miss Molly again, admit it.' Archie shouted to Julian as he walked to the door.

'Well, I am certainly in no hurry to see Mrs Creswell again, but the end justifies the means.'

12

Juniper's eyes flitted from Archibald to Julian and back again throughout the dinner. Cecily had lavished them with a dish of roasted peacock. This was an impressive centre piece, although Molly looked at the dead bird's raised head with an element of sadness because in life it had been truly a thing of beauty.

Juniper enjoyed making small talk, whilst Cecily steered the conversation from one topic to another should she tire of the current one. She watched carefully how the group was interacting. Molly tried on occasion to put a different point of view across but both women would talk her discreetly down, so she ate in silence, only nodding and smiling as and when it was appropriate.

Julian was being careful also. He looked mainly at Cecily and Juniper, answering questions and asking some of them himself. He almost appeared to pay Molly little or no interest at all.

It was Archibald who addressed her, much to Juniper's surprise. 'Miss Mason, what was your father's business?'

'He was a shoemaker, sir,' she answered humbly and was instantly corrected by Cecily.

'Nathan was much more than that. He was a master of his craft and owned two manufactories. He supplied some of your own officers with the finest boots. Indeed, he was a true craftsman and entrepreneur.' Her face was slightly flushed and she looked down at her empty glass.

Molly saw Julian's expression; she was either an excellent actress or the outburst had been one of what appeared to be genuine affection. 'Yes, he was, ma'am. I did not mean to belittle him but he was humble above all else and would never have boasted — even if he had good reason to.'

'You are quite right, Mary. However,

we can do it for him now in his sad absence.' Cecily looked directly at Molly and, for a second, the ice in her eyes had melted.

'Your father, Mr Creswell, was so different. He was an educated and cultured gentleman. You must miss him a lot, sir,' Juniper said in a sweet innocent voice. Molly could see that the effort was lost on Julian. He was a grieving man who knew only too well what type of man his father had been.

'He was everything a son could wish for, Juniper. I am happy to note that you appreciated him. It will have made his life so much fuller,' Julian answered and smiled at her, but his eyes, Molly noted had hardened.

'More wine!' Cecily ordered, and a servant dutifully obeyed, filling up each glass in turn, although Molly's had only been sipped. Juniper, however, had emptied hers as had Cecily and Archibald.

What seemed to Molly many hours later, the men were eventually left to take their port and the women adjourned to the room adjacent.

Juniper waited until the door was closed by the maid and then faced her mother with a glowing face, and beamed widely at them. 'Mama isn't he just divine? He looks so . . . grown, in stature and character. Do you know, I really think the war has been good for him? He hardly took his eyes off me — so did Julian.' Juniper sat down on the cream sofa next to the fire and sighed contentedly. 'I am so full of happiness to be admired so,' she admitted.

'I believe you could be right, Juniper,' Cecily said, and then glanced at Molly who had sat down on the hard wooden chair by the card table. 'What do you think of his friend, Mr Julian Creswell?'

'I don't really know what to think of him, ma'am, because he has hardly spoken to me all evening.' Molly saw Juniper smile at her mother, obviously feeling she had scored a victory of some sort over Molly.

'Perhaps your lack of social graces has not impressed him, girl,' Cecily replied. 'I shall encourage him to take you for a walk tomorrow. Perhaps then you might be able to make some kind of impression upon him. It might be advantageous to you if you could engage his interest. You never know, he may even take pity on you, as his friend is ready to marry — it could place the idea in his mind. Remember he has been at war and, worse still, a prisoner. Show him a kind understanding nature and he will be drawn into your arms and you into his heart. To put it plainly, Mary, he is ripe for the picking so tomorrow start reaping in your harvest. If you don't care for the inn-keeper's son then make a play for the soldier. He is a better catch.' Cecily stared at her pointedly. 'For once swallow that pride of yours and take my advice.' Cecily slipped off her shoe and rubbed her foot, warming it in the heat from the fire. 'They will not be long. They have promised to play cards with us before retiring to bed.'

'Won't five be an odd number?' asked Juniper.

'Oh yes, you're quite right,' Cecily agreed and looked directly at Molly.

Molly nodded to Cecily. 'Perhaps you could pass on my apologies to the gentlemen, because I am tired and would like to retire myself.' Molly stood up after excusing herself.

Cecily was obviously pleased that she had obeyed the silent request for her to make herself scarce. 'Good girl, we shall tell you all about our evening tomorrow, but not early as I suspect the evening will be long and enjoyable. Enjoy your rest, girl.'

Molly nodded, trying to look downcast rather than relieved, and made her way to the door but then turned and looked over to Cecily. 'Thank you for the coat and the advice. I shall treasure both.'

Cecily's expression showed that she appreciated the words. Molly climbed the stairs reflecting on what had been another eventful day. As she ascended she saw the door open to the dining room and Julian slip outside crossing the hall to her. He stood by her placing his hand over hers as it rested on the banister. 'Where are you going?' he mouthed silently.

'To bed,' she mouthed back, grinning widely at his clandestine manner.

'Where is your room?' His mouth framed the words perfectly.

'Next door but one to yours, sir. Why should you ask?' she replied in kind.

He winked at her, took a step back, bowed low and slipped back into the room. She shook her head at his manner. He was far more mature and knowledgeable than her. Alice had warned him, Molly was sure of that. She just hoped that the warning had been heeded. He apparently found her attractive, as she certainly did him, but let him take advantage of her she certainly would not. It was more than she dare risk. The street was a cold, dark and lonely place to be turned out onto for a fallen woman. Then she remembered her money at Mrs Arndale's. She could always be the baker's apprentice; she liked the idea no matter how impractical it was.

13

Molly had not only retired but had gone to sleep when the handle of her bedchamber door turned slowly and silently. Julian entered the room and tiptoed over to her bed. The first she knew of his presence was when a hand gently cradled her lips.

Automatically, she clenched her fist into a ball and struck out. Still in her half asleep state she had given no thought as to who the intruder could be.

He caught her small fist in the palm of his hand and was stifling a laugh. Her eyes were open wide now. Julian whispered gently, 'It is only me, Molly. Do not fear . . . And please do not hurt me.' He removed his hand from her face and released her fingers from his.

'Is that knowledge supposed to make me feel safer? You are a stranger — a man — in my bedchamber. What do you think you are doing here, and why?' Her voice was spoken in a vexed whisper.

'Acting shamefully, no doubt, and risking receiving a beating from a rolling pin around my ears, should you inform Mrs Arndale of my nerve and arrogance.' He grinned at her. In the half light from the low fire that still burned in the hearth she could see his impish smile. He had crouched down by the side of the bed, his face only inches from hers. 'Would it help if I told you on my honour that I respect you greatly and, despite the proximity of your beautiful body, I wish only to talk — to whisper to you?'

She turned her head to face his. 'Do you have any honour?' she asked innocently. 'You have showed little since I have met you.'

'I am wounded . . . deeply wounded at your inference, miss. I could have taken liberties with you in the alley, but I protected you, your reputation and your honour.' His voice, still low, was filled with mockery.

'You stole a kiss,' she added.

'You gave it willingly enough,' he replied.

'You are insolent. You wish to talk to me about what, sir?' She knew she could not deny it for she had lingered a while in his embrace.

'Call me Julian, please.' His normal manner returned.

'Julian, that would be improper in the extreme,' she replied.

'Then be daring and risqué. I wish to know why I am carrying a key for you. Why did you trust me with it and what does it unlock?' He showed her the key which he had placed on a chain around his neck. 'What was in the note, Molly?'

'You have many questions. I trust you because I trust my own judgement of people. You will guard it for me, and I need you, your muscle and your honour to retrieve what it opens. Here, before you expire of curiosity, you may read the note.' She leaned over and pulled the piece of vellum from the embroidered pouch which she kept under her pillow. 'Read it for yourself, Julian.'

He did, but then shrugged his shoulders as he was clearly none the wiser as to what it referred. 'So where is this place that the pair of you shared?'

'Cecily asked that too,' she answered propping her head up on her hand. Her hair fell loose over her shoulders and she saw his eyes survey her as the sheet and quilted cover fell back revealing her nightdress to her waist. Although she was covered by the fine white cotton he looked at her as though his mind had removed it as a barrier to her body beneath.

'And what did you reply?' he asked absently, as he wrapped a lock of her hair around his finger.

'I told her that the place that I could find my father was in my heart,' she said simply, and his eyes focussed directly on hers, a smile crossing his face.

'Then I hold the key to your heart?'

She stifled a giggle. 'In a manner of speaking, yes, you do. But, although it is a pleasant enough thought, it was a lie. Tomorrow you need to take me for a ride in a gig or phaeton. Choose something that is quick and can handle a rutted road surface. Can you bring a spade and something to use as a lever?'

He nodded to her, 'We are going on a treasure hunt, you and I?' He shook his head. 'I shall do as you bid, my dearest Mary.'

'Molly, I like to be called Molly.'

'Molly then, but as I am to be of use to you tomorrow may I be granted the pleasure of saying goodnight to you now?' he asked, his mouth only a couple of inches from her own.

'You may say what you wish, Julian,' she replied, intending to comment that it was what he wanted to do that would be stopped, but before her words were complete, his hand cupped the back of her head, bringing her lips to his. He kissed her tenderly, but then with a growing passion. Before she knew what was happening he had lifted her body to his, the other arm wrapping itself around her, his hand finding her lower back. She felt the warmth of his embrace against the cool of the night air. The dying fire held no competition for the heat that rose within her. She knew she should pull away and stop him, but she liked him, his touch and realised that it was more than that, for she had started to fall in love with him; she who had decided not to marry; never to be hurt or widowed. He had come into her life so suddenly yet she felt that, when she was with him, she was happy and alive.

His hand slid up her body from the small of her back to her ribs and inched slowly around to her side. He placed his hand over the curve of her body; a thin fabric being the only barrier between the flesh of his hand and her breast. It was then he stopped kissing her and sighed deeply. He removed his hand and embraced her, holding her tightly in his arms. Julian kissed her forehead.

He seemed flustered, his breath uneven. He leaned across and picked up the quilted cover from the bed, wrapping it around her shoulders.

'You didn't heed Alice's words very well, did you?' she asked him, her face also flushed.

'I did, but you are so special, young lady.' He kissed her cheeks before releasing her. 'I will not take advantage of you. I have behaved badly. I cannot apologise, for I have delighted in every moment and regret that I must stop where we are. I give you my word that I shall not indulge myself again.' He released her and stepped away, but she held onto his hand and pulled him back.

'Not even if I am willing to be indulged?' she asked, somewhat brazenly, and saw the joy in his face.

He stroked her hair. 'You are playing with fire, miss. Take care.'

'Would you burn me, sir?' she asked, as she rested her head upon his chest.

'No, I would never hurt you. I shall

have to protect you, though, for you have little restraint with me and that is a devilish temptation you open to my heart. I shall keep all others away and shall make proper advances to you. I shall court you and win your heart.' He stepped back this time, and she let him go. 'We shall come to know each other properly, Molly, and then, if we like what we learn of each other, I will . . . ' He looked slightly nervous at the realisation of where his conversation was leading him. She could not help but smile at him for his manner had an appeal of its own, to Molly. 'We shall see when the time is right. Goodnight, Molly.' He blew her a kiss and left silently.

14

Archibald waited patiently for a chance of a solitary moment with Juniper to have her to himself for a moment or two. Cecily finally decided to retire and he tried not to show how relieved he was that Juniper lingered a while. Julian, like the good friend he was, followed after her.

Cecily turned and looked at her daughter who was still talking to Archibald. 'Are you coming to bed, dear?' she asked patiently.

'Yes, Mama,' she answered and stood up. That was sufficient a gesture for Cecily to respectfully leave the room with Julian.

The door idly closed behind her and Archibald wasted no time; he stood next to Juniper taking her hand in his and lifting it up to his lips. Instantly, she turned her face to his and looked up into his eyes. He had difficulty in pushing the images of the night before away from his memory. For the girl, Sally, was full of confidence and spirit and had more than met his desire and appetite in the bedchamber. She had so much energy, and abandon, that he had revelled in the indulgence and had found the previous hours in Juniper's company stifling by comparison and, if he were honest, boring in the extreme. Not that he wanted to marry a whore, but a woman of warmth who could share her love with him. There was something he had to know, though, and that was a simple test. What was Juniper like to kiss? Did her passion spill over and set them both on fire or did she never stop talking long enough to give her mouth a chance to find another purpose.

'Archibald!' she let out a little gasp, and flushed slightly as she looked at the door, as if in fear that her mother would return and find the two lovers in a compromising situation.

'Juniper, I have longed to be alone

with you if only for a few precious moments. Let us not waste them.' He gently pulled her to him and embraced her. He kissed her on her lips gently and she stifled a giggle, which he found most off-putting.

He lifted his head away from hers and looked at her.

'Archibald!' she said and smiled.

'Kiss me, Juniper, as if you really want me to kiss you.' He was looking at her eyes, hoping for a sign of desire.

'Of course I want you, you dote. Once we are married there will be plenty of time for that sort of thing,' she answered, and then as if she realised he was not that impressed by her coyness, she closed her eyes and pursed her lips so that he would kiss her again with her permission.

He did. This time he lingered and his kiss became more urgent, more intrusive, but she did not reciprocate. Instead, she pushed him gently away. 'Archibald, that is enough for now, you shall have more . . . ' she lowered her eyelashes slightly, 'you shall have everything you desire, once we are wed. However, for now, my darling Archibald, I must retire. I do not wish you to think me easy, Archibald. I am not that kind of girl.'

'We are to marry, Juniper . . . what harm can it do?'

'Precisely, so you will have to wait and be the gentleman that I know you to be.'

He released her. 'Yes, you are quite right.'

'Mother will be suspicious if I do not go up.' She walked to the door and smiled back at him. 'Perhaps we should speed the arrangements up seeing as you are so . . . keen.' She giggled and left the room.

When Julian re-entered the room some half an hour later Archibald was still standing with his hands on the mantelpiece and staring into the fire, watching the flames slowly die away.

'Do you not wish to go to bed tonight, Archie? Or are you so love

134

struck that you are truly mesmerised,' Julian asked and flopped down on the sofa next to him.

Archibald stood straight and looked at his friend. 'Help me, Jules. Her passion is like that fire, dead or nearly dying. What am I to do? She is so changed.'

'No, Archie, it is you who is so changed. You have woken up and seen her for what she is. You have experienced women — mature, experienced women, and that girl is no match for them. You need to give her a chance. She has been raised under the shadow of the woman, Cecily . . . Juniper is naïve. You cannot compare her to the whore whose bed you left hours since. Juniper has been well bred, and you must accept the rules of courtship. We are not in the army now.'

★ ★ ★

Although the door was slightly ajar, neither man heard the girl gasp as she listened to them talk. She had not heard Archibald come up to his room, but someone had ventured back down. Thinking it might be her mama she had opened the door to her bedchamber, but instead she saw the back of Julian descending. Curiosity had overtaken her sense of propriety, so she had dared to venture down in her nightgown to see if Archibald had fallen asleep in the chair, or if he was displeased with her.

When she heard Archibald's opening comment to Julian, her heart felt as though it had been stabbed. He was so arrogant, she thought. What did he want from her? Was she supposed to act like a loose woman, however that may be. No, she would not lower her standards for any man.

She placed a hand to her mouth to stifle a sob which threatened to escape her and ran tearfully back to her room. Her hero had been with some little whore in her own town whilst she had waited anxiously for him to arrive fresh from his war and into her arms.

Was he like the men who had treated her mama so ill? Well, he would not use her and leave her like Creswell and the Mason man. Juniper flopped back down on the bed and smiled. Her mother needed no man; she had herself to look after her. No, Lt. Cherry would honour his obligations. He would marry Juniper and give her children, then he could go wherever he wanted to. She did not need a man; she wanted children and needed money and respectability. He would pay for the insult — or rather the whore would if she found out who the wanton creature was.

★ ★ ★

The men, oblivious to the fact that their conversation had been overheard, continued, 'Compare Juniper to the other woman, Mary. There is no comparison, Julian. One is reserved whilst the other is full of her own emptiness — if that makes any sense to you.'

Julian smiled at him. 'Yes, it makes

perfect sense, but that is because the child has not experienced life beyond a shop and a small circle of friends. What do you expect? Poor Archie,' he answered unsympathetically with a glint of happiness showing in his own eyes.

At first Archibald did not look at his friend and could not see the man's change of countenance. 'It is just I don't know how she will cope with me. She needs an unscarred man on the inside as well as the outside. Juniper would be better suited to a pretty boy fresh from university — full of ideas and air.' He glanced at his friend as no response was forthcoming. 'You rascal!' Archie exclaimed as the truth dawned on him. 'You have your eyes set on Mary.'

'Molly is a fine woman. I find her attractive in person and in looks. Besides, she needs my help.' He grinned broadly, happy at the thought of a courtship with his new found friend.

'And you will give it to her willingly.'

Archibald folded his arms and looked at his contented friend.

'Yes, I shall for I like her very much.'

'And you, the man who did not believe in love at first sight, the biggest cynic of Wellington's army, has fallen in love. Yet it is my marriage we are supposed to be celebrating.'

'You forget, Archie, that I'm not a soldier any more. A soldier who limps when he runs is no use as a skirmisher whether he is an officer or a foot soldier.' Julian's manner was serious all of a sudden.

'Then be glad that you have found a woman to retire with. That is if she can tolerate you. Now go to your own bed and think about how tomorrow you can unravel the truth of this mess. I still think the woman wore her men down. Murder is a fanciful notion of a grieving son, Julian. Accept the fact and soon, or you will make a damn fool of yourself. Put your brain to better use helping me so that I may possibly escape a life of ear damage listening to an empty gong resounding in my head.'

Archibald downed the glass of port which had been left on the table and abandoned Julian to his own sweet or troubled thoughts.

15

Molly arose early the next morning and went down to the kitchens to make herself a light snack. She was excited at the prospect of going out on her journey with Julian, although she realised he may want to sleep in as he had stayed up to drink and play cards. Molly was happy, she was filled with a strange feeling that her future would not be as lonely as her past.

The kitchen was already warm and the table was covered with flour. Molly was surprised as she had expected it to be still clear from the night before. The maid would not usually bake so early in the day. She would be stoking fires and warming the house for when the mistress awoke. Molly looked at the mess on the flagstone floor; this was so unlike her. This behaviour was very unusual.

Molly heard noises coming from the larder and was surprised when it was Juniper who emerged with a bowl in her arms in which lay a large ball of dough.

'What on earth are you doing down here, Juniper?' Molly asked as the girl slammed the bowl down on the old oak table.

'I'm making one of my special loaves. It is what I do when I am annoyed and want to hit something. I make dough and I mangle it until I'm not vexed anymore! It releases anger that otherwise might call a flux or an ague,' she snapped her answer back at Molly who was intrigued by her actions and outburst of temper.

'Then why are you so vexed?' Molly looked at the open fire and the hearth. 'Juniper, we don't have a bread oven.' Molly sat down away from the fury of fist punching and kneading that was being inflicted upon the hapless dough.

'I know that. I'll give it to the girl at the baker's shop. Your baker-woman lets people use her oven for their own dough if she is paid for the trouble.' Juniper finished moulding the dough to the shape she required and looked at it contentedly obviously pleased that she had done a good job.

'Why are you so vexed, Juniper? I thought you should be so happy this morning. Archibald has grown into a fine man.' Molly looked at the girl's eyes. They were bloodshot. She had either cried a lot or she was very tired.

'I don't think you would understand. You cannot judge a man on just what he looks like or what he says.' She sniffed and covered the dough with a piece of moist muslin, then looked knowingly at Molly. 'It's what they do that counts!'

'Well I won't understand if you don't confide in me. Has he done something to you that you did not like?' Molly asked gently.

'You'd love me to say he had, wouldn't you? Then you can laugh at my misfortune,' Juniper snapped at her again.

143

'I would not do that not if it was so serious as to upset you so,' Molly reasoned.

Juniper cleaned her hands and left the mess for the maid to clean up. 'Well, I'm sorry to disappoint you for he has hardly done anything to me. I am not that sort of girl. I have standards and I'm no fool. No, he shall not do anything to me unless I am married to him.' She breathed deeply as if she was considering what she should say next. 'It is just that I . . . I am unsure of what Archibald will expect of me,' Juniper said a little coyly, her manner changed.

'Has your mother not talked to you of personal things?' Molly asked, not really feeling that she had the experience needed to advise the girl.

'Sort of, but I don't know what I'm supposed to feel, if anything.' Juniper was definitely flustered, but Molly was not certain she was being completely honest. Why would curiosity and the normal doubts that every betrothed girl faced make her vexed? Nervous perhaps but not vexed.

Molly thought for a moment. 'Excited, warm . . . I suppose.' Molly looked at her and shrugged not wanting to explain how she could know for sure. The feelings were still so new and recent to her, but very real.

'Well, where does the girl live, or should I take this down to the baker's myself?' Juniper looked at the results of her labour with contentment showing that at least she was pleased with her loaf.

'Are you sure you know how to make one?' Molly stared at the dough thinking that it looked like Alice's, but Juniper never did menial work.

'We were not always moneyed, Molly. There was a time when Mother had no maid of her own. My father owned a smallholding. He farmed and, like Mother's mother before her, we grew our own food and made our own dough. No, it was only when Father dug up a small hoard of coin that things changed. However, he did not live much beyond that and so Mother and I changed our lives for the better. I only do this when I feel the need — or knead.' She laughed at her own quip.

'You can't go to Sally's home, Juniper. Cecily would have a turn if you went anywhere near the inn.' Molly laughed at the thought, glad that the girl's spirit had lifted slightly.

'The inn? What's she doing there?' Juniper stared at Molly.

'She works there evenings, and has a room there in the back.' Molly grinned a little to herself. 'She serves drinks and beyond that I am not sure, but she makes her living from doing odd jobs.'

'Does she now!' Juniper said, and smiled. 'What of her family?'

'She doesn't have any. Her father was killed in the war and her mother died giving birth to another child. That is why she is as she is, I suppose,' Molly explained.

'Really! Well I shall have my bread baked. I'll tell the maid to take it down and the girl to bring it back to me when it is done. I'll give her a coin for that and a special treat seeing as her life is so hard and empty. Must be terrible having no one to care about you.' She dropped her apron on the chair and yawned. 'I think I shall be able to sleep now.'

'Don't worry about, Sally; her life is seldom empty and she has lots of friends,' Molly said, and chuckled to herself.

Juniper looked back at her in her usual patronising manner. 'Really, Molly, you can be so uncaring at times.'

Molly shook her head before finding herself some food. Juniper, she thought, changed her moods like the wind changed direction. The maid appeared at the kitchen doorway in a foul temper.

'Honestly, miss, if I didn't have enough to do already, what with guests and the like, and now Miss Juniper expects me to go cavorting about town at this hour!' She sighed and saw the mess on her table. 'Oh Lord, what has she been doing?'

'Never mind that, I'll clean this up. You go do your errand before you're in trouble,' Molly said, as she picked up the apron and wrapped it around herself.

'You are a love. For goodness sake don't get caught doing my work or I'll be in a deal of trouble — and you, for that matter.'

'Go on with you. I'm waiting for Mr Creswell to rise anyway,' Molly said absently.

'Oh are you?' The maid grinned at the statement, but then added, 'You best hurry then because he's breakfasted already and is reading a book in the morning room. It looks like he couldn't sleep for thinking about something, or someone perhaps.' She giggled as she pulled on her coat.

'Be gone with you woman!' Molly shouted in an angry voice but the maid just laughed, knowing that Molly was a 'good sort' and not at all like the other two household females.

16

Molly quickly cleaned up Juniper's mess. She wiped the table down but was annoyed when she spiked her finger on a grass seed. The girl was useless, Molly thought.

Once finished, she looked at her reflection in the old looking glass. She was pleased that she still appeared respectable despite her unexpected chore, and so made her way calmly to the morning room.

Julian stood up as soon as she entered. He was wearing his knee boots over his trousers. His long waistcoat was practical. His rather cavalier appearance suited him more than the restrictive dinner suit he had worn the previous evening. He looked relaxed and his face showed nothing but pleasure at her arrival.

Molly had chosen her most comfortable walking dress. She wanted to wear her long coat and bonnet, and had chosen a pair of sturdy boots. Looking at the freedom his costume afforded him, she wished she, too, could wear breeches.

His smile faded slightly as she approached him.

'Good morning, Molly. Are you not happy to see me this morning . . . you look a little pensive. Should I be apologising?'

She walked straight up to him and on tiptoe she stretched up in order to kiss his cheek quickly. 'Whatever for? Apologise for nothing, for it is I who acted badly.' She grinned at him, as the smile returned to his face. 'I was merely thinking that I am jealous that you can wear breeches and I cannot. I wish I could, for then I could ride and climb with ease. They are so practical, unlike long skirts.'

He laughed at her comments.

'Do I shock you?' she asked, realising her mouth had spoken without her brain thinking beforehand, again.

'No, not shock; I was just visualising you in breeches also and thinking it would be a sight I would not mind seeing for myself.' He shook his head as if dismissing the thought. 'Now, to more serious matters, have you eaten yet?' he asked, as he reached for her hand and raised it to his lips, kissing it once. 'I told you I shall treat you as a lady.'

She shrugged her shoulders. 'Yes, I ate in the kitchen before cleaning up Juniper's mess.' Molly did not know why she should share this information with him, other than she was still vexed with the girl for causing such a fuss.

'Her mess?' he repeated, as he put on his greatcoat.

'Yes, she made bread this morning to let out some of her anger. Did you or Archibald upset her last night?' She collected her own coat and bonnet from the hall. It seemed to be the most natural thing in the world to be going out with this man who was yet so new to her.

151

'I do not believe so. I cannot imagine Juniper in a kitchen let alone making a bread loaf.' He held her coat up so that she could slip easily into it. 'No matter, we should make our way. I have a gig at the corner of the row of houses. Should we promenade, miss?' He lifted his elbow to her so that she could hook her hand under his arm. She smiled up at him, not able to act with pomp or propriety. She was happy and she knew it showed. What is more, so was he, and that was the thing that made him special for they were not afraid to show their feelings to each other.

He opened the front door and they were about to step outside when Cecily's voice surprised them.

'When shall we expect you two back or are you going to surprise us?' Their faces sobered, but Cecily's was full of good humour, it appeared.

'Ma'am, we thought everyone was still abed after the excesses of yesterevening. We could not sleep longer as the day is so sunny, so Mr Creswell asked me to take some fresh air with him before everyone arose,' Molly answered confidently.

'Now you are awake, Cecily, perhaps you would care to join us also?' Julian's face showed no sign of insincerity as he addressed the woman.

She looked very pleased at the offer. 'Julian, you are so kind. However, I must decline for I have not broken my fast and you youngsters have so much more energy than I. No, you two walk out together, and enjoy yourselves. I shall wait here for Juniper and Archibald to arise.'

'Juniper was up earlier, I met her in the kitchen, but she returned to her slumber.'

'Whatever were you both doing in the kitchens, Mary?' Cecily said, looking her usual vexed self.

'I went to find some food, ma'am, and found Juniper baking.'

Cecily shook her head. 'It is amazing what excited young girls get up to. You must excuse their manners, Mr Creswell.

Run along.' Cecily turned around and retraced her steps up the stairs.

It was with great relief that Molly found herself approaching the gig with just Julian by her side. 'Whatever were you thinking of? If she'd said yes, would you have sat her on the horse?' Molly looked up at him but he was not at all concerned.

'She would not come with us. She thinks I am out to get as much from her and this house as I can. If you were a part of my vengeance and greed then she would leave you to make of me what you will. If I prove to be a rat, she has bought time to work out how to keep my hands from her business, whilst I humour myself with you and she has lost nothing — but you, everything. So why would she stand in my way?' He lifted her up to the seat in the gig. Whilst his hands were still upon her waist she looked deep into his eyes. 'Are you toying with me?' she asked quietly.

'Think, woman! What has happened

between us and what could have, should I have willed it so. Ponder what I have told you and answer the question for yourself.' He spoke matter-of-factly, then climbed into his seat beside her and flicked the reins.

Once they were away from the town and on the open road he looked down at her. 'Are you still thinking?'

'You are a strange man, Julian.'

'How many have you known to compare me with?' he asked in good humour.

'You are a good man. Where are you taking me now?'

'To the main road; after that, nowhere unless you give me directions.' He placed an arm around her and she leaned in to his body.

'Before you get to the road, take the turning to the right that leads into the woods.' She watched in silence as the familiar turning approached.

17

Cecily stormed upstairs and into Juniper's bedchamber. The body in the bed was sound asleep but Cecily pulled back the quilted cover and woke her daughter up. She opened the heavy drapes.

'Juniper, Juniper.' She shook her shoulder, and the bleary eyed girl woke up.

'What is it? Whatever has happened?' She focussed on her mother's concerned face.

'What have you done?'

Juniper rubbed her eyes and squinted at the bright light that was flooding into the room.

'Nothing, I've been asleep I . . . ' she stared at her mother whose eyes were close to tears.

'You baked that bread again, haven't you?' Cecily looked at her and the girl glanced away.

'I only made a loaf.' She held onto her mother's arm. 'He's been sleeping with a whore, Mama. He compared me to her. I heard him talking last night with Julian.' She sniffed.

'You promised, Juniper. No more antics. If a man slept with a whore before he weds, what of it? He isn't going to expect a wife to be like one. Foolish girl! What have you done with it?' Cecily stood up.

'I sent it to the baker's. We don't have an oven here,' Juniper said sulkily.

'What in hell's name did I ever do to deserve you?' She shook her head. 'Your possessiveness will be the fall of us both.'

The girl was now sobbing. 'I didn't want him to hurt me like Pa hurt you,' she blubbered.

'Listen, Juniper, and listen well.' Cecily held her daughter by her upper arms making her stare into her eyes. 'Your father was a bully, he paid for the years of abuse he caused us both and we are free of him. You do not need to do the same thing to a good man. Don't ever do it again!' Cecily shook the frightened girl. 'Promise me, Juniper,' she added.

'I'm sorry, I was angry and scared.' Juniper looked at her mother. 'I didn't mean it for Archie, I wanted to make the whore suffer,' Juniper explained as if that was reasonable.

'Don't you think that a whore suffers enough in her own pitiful existence?' Cecily asked, and saw that Juniper had never given the matter a second thought. 'Dress and I shall have it retrieved and you behave, Juniper.'

Cecily left the house running towards the bakery when she saw Julian and Molly together on the gig.

'Damnation!' she muttered, 'What in hell are those two up to?' Quickly she turned back to the house.

★　★　★

The gig was stopped outside a boarded up cottage amidst an overgrown garden.

'What is this place?' Julian asked as he helped her down.

'This was my home, my family home.' Molly happily ran down the path to the door.

Brushing away a runner from a bramble she turned the door handle only to find that a lock had been fitted and there was no key.

'Do you require this?' he held the key up behind her.

'Yes, I think so, if I am right it will be a perfect fit.'

She turned the key and opened the door. The cottage was spacious inside and empty, yet still had a strong homely feel to it.

They stood looking at the empty hearth where once a pot hung down on an iron chain.

'I still love this place,' Molly said, and looked around the empty rooms.

'So why did I need a spade or a crowbar?' he asked.

She smiled, and led him back to the room that had been her mother and father's. 'Here,' she pointed to the slab of stone by the empty fire grate, 'You need to lift this one. Father kept things under it.'

Julian did as he was bid. She watched as he lifted up one of the stone flags. Surely enough, beneath it was a hollowed compartment hiding a leather document wallet.

He removed it and handed it to Molly who grinned excitedly. 'You're strong like my father was,' she said as he replaced the piece of stone.

'Molly, I'm not that strong . . . I was injured. My leg snapped and now I cannot run without hobbling.'

Molly looked up and saw his flushed face. He swallowed as it had obviously been a difficult thing for him to admit. She walked over to him. 'I'm sorry.' She kissed his cheek gently.

'They broke it deliberately when I was a prisoner. It is why I am left with the problem.'

'Julian, I am sorry for you that it happened but it does not make you any less of a man in my eyes. I think it is the inner scars that need time to heal with you.'

'Yes, I think you are right.' He bent down and kissed her lips then pulled away. 'See what you do to me? I forget myself already.'

She smiled and opened the wallet. Within it were the deeds of the cottage, the owner named as herself as a dowry present. She pulled out more moneyed notes, leaving her the key to her independence that she had craved. She looked up at Julian.

'You do not need a man to provide for you,' he said, almost dolefully.

'I think it is better when one wants someone more than needs,' she looked up into his eyes. 'It is a healthier bond for a relationship do you not agree?' Molly removed a letter. It was scribbled in her father's hand. She held it in her own and read it out aloud.

My dear Molly,
I leave you this precious place and

all its loving memories. You shall now have achieved your majority. If you are wed I wish you years of happiness. If you are not then I ask you why not? Consider the young man who I hope will have brought the key to you. He is the son of a good, but fallen man.

Molly, I owe Mrs Creswell an apology on two accounts. Firstly, I once suspected her of an evil act against my friend but came to learn he had an illness no man should contract from a sinful woman and one no woman should be given. Still, Cecily forgave him and nursed him through his madness to his end.

Secondly, I owe her an apology for I never gave her the privilege of having my name. We never married, Molly. When I returned with her from Harrogate, we had become as man and wife but we never committed ourselves legally to each other. I knew my health was fading, my heart was *big but not strong, so I sold the businesses and let her invest the money in her shop, so long as she looked after your well being. Our home I kept for you.*

I know she is not your mother but she has tried to be.

God bless,

Your loving father.

'So now you know the truth of it!' Cecily's voice surprised them once more. She held a riding crop in her hand. 'He never found the time to say those words to me.'

'So that is why you used my father's name,' Julian said.

'Yes, he was a good man. I loved him, but I don't suppose you would believe that. Juniper's father was unkind, but your father was not. He already had the illness when we met, but we were good friends, he and I.'

Julian and Molly looked at each other guiltily.

'We thought . . . ' Molly began then

stopped as Cecily put her hand in the air.

'No matter. It is done. What will you do now, girl? Become the 'baker's apprentice'?' she laughed at the thought, 'or live here, or stay with us?'

'I will make this place liveable again,' she looked at Julian, 'if you will help me?' she asked, and then added, 'I don't want to be anyone's apprentice.'

He nodded and took hold of her hand. 'I could live here whilst you stay in the house until the home is ready to be shared by a family again.' He lifted an eyebrow and smiled as she was already nodding her agreement.

'Good, we shall have two weddings, possibly, then,' Cecily said emphatically.

'Cecily, Juniper and Archibald need time if they are to make a good decision. Neither is ready for the other yet.' Julian's voice was authoritative, and Molly was surprised when Cecily nodded her agreement. There was an air of resignation about the woman that was strange.

'I know, they shall have as much time as they need. Juniper is still very young; she will mature, in time.' Cecily swallowed.

Molly walked over to her. 'The bread, there was seed by it . . . what was in it?' she asked the woman calmly.

'It is done. The dough was burned.' She looked at Molly straight in the eye. 'It is no more, the girl was confused.'

She turned to face Julian. 'I have a business to run, your business, as it happens for that is where your father's money was invested. So if you will excuse me I shall return to it. You may see the accounts whenever your solicitor wishes, Julian. There is nothing to hide.'

'No matter, ma'am. I have my own means. You keep the shop.'

Cecily nodded and left them alone.

Molly faced Julian. 'Do you think Juniper is sick?' she asked.

'Whatever Juniper is her mother has made her and she will handle her. As for Archie, I shall discuss things with him, only time will tell.'

He pulled her to him and embraced her, letting his kiss increase in passion and their bodies respond to each other freely.

She pulled away slightly and laughed. 'What happened to restraint, Mr Creswell?'

'You have given me the key,' he said simply, as he held her gently in his arms, 'to your home, where your heart is, and where soon I shall be also if it is your will that it should be so.'

Molly hugged him knowing that in this lovely peaceful place they would both be able to love and heal whilst rebuilding a new home together.

THE END

Other titles in the
Linford Romance Library:

PALE ORCHID

Mavis Thomas

Bethany delays her hopes of rescuing a failing relationship while she helps a friend by working at The Corner Cattery. But there are unexpected problems. She becomes involved with twin brothers and the bitter feud between them: Dominic the successful but troubled and moody playwright; Darryl the dedicated doctor torn between his work in Africa and his two motherless children. Many conflicts must be resolved, and searching questions answered, before Bethany can see clearly her road ahead.